# kids
# like
# US

# kids like US

## HILARY REYL

SQUARE
FISH

**FARRAR STRAUS GIROUX**
NEW YORK

SQUARE
FISH

An imprint of Macmillan Publishing Group, LLC
175 Fifth Avenue, New York, NY 10010
fiercereads.com

Square Fish and the Square Fish logo are trademarks of Macmillan
and are used by Farrar Straus Giroux under license from Macmillan.

Our books may be purchased in bulk for promotional, educational, or
business use. Please contact your local bookseller or the Macmillan
Corporate and Premium Sales Department at (800) 221-7945 ext. 5442
or by email at MacmillanSpecialMarkets@macmillan.com.

Library of Congress Cataloging-in-Publication Data

Names: Reyl, Hilary, author.
Title: Kids like us / Hilary Reyl.
Description: New York : Farrar Straus Giroux, 2017. | Summary: "A tender,
    smart, and romantic YA novel about a teenage boy on the autism spectrum
    who learns he is capable of love"—Provided by publisher. |
Identifiers: LCCN 2016058778 (print) | LCCN 2017024712 (ebook) |
    ISBN 978-1-250-18069-8 (paperback)       ISBN 978-0-374-30630-4 (ebook)
Subjects: | CYAC: Autism—Fiction. | Love—Fiction.
Classification: LCC PZ7.1.R485 (ebook) | LCC PZ7.1.R485 Ki 2017 (print) |
    DDC [Fic]—dc23
LC record available at https://lccn.loc.gov/2016058778

Originally published in the United States by Farrar Straus Giroux
First Square Fish edition, 2018
Book designed by Elizabeth H. Clark
Square Fish logo designed by Filomena Tuosto

1   3   5   7   9   10   8   6   4   2

LEXILE: 700L / AR: 4.9

*This book is for my sister, Eleanor O'Neill,*

*from her biggest fan*

# kids
# like
# US

# Tuesday, May 17
## 4:35 p.m.

Yesterday, you, Mom, and Elisabeth landed in Paris, France. You have never been here before.

Today, you are speeding through the French countryside. You are a sixteen-year-old boy named Martin on a one-hour-and-two-minute train ride from the Gare Montparnasse in Paris to a town in the Loire Valley, where there are many famous castles. Here is a list of the major castles: Amboise, Blois, Chambord, Chenonceau, Chinon, Langeais, and Villandry.

The town where you are headed is called Saint-Pierre-des-Corps. In Saint-Pierre-des-Corps, you will board a slower train that makes three stops before it takes you to your final destination of the town of Chenonceaux, where you will find the most beautiful castle of all. The name of the town is spelled with an *x* at the end, and the name of the castle has no *x*. This shows that they are not the same thing.

This second train ride, between Saint-Pierre-des-Corps and Chenonceaux, will last twenty-one minutes.

You, Mom, and Elisabeth are in seats forty-seven, forty-eight, and forty-nine. Seats forty-seven and forty-eight are on one side of a table and seats forty-nine and fifty are on the opposite side. There is no one in seat fifty. You are in seat forty-nine, facing Elisabeth and Mom. You are next to no one.

You have never seen so many sunflowers through a window. They are all turned the same way, to face the light.

You are nervous and excited. This summer in France is a chance for you to become someone else. Someone you were meant to be. Even though you have always spoken French with your father, you have only visited this country in your head. Maybe the actual place will unlock you.

You aren't supposed to dream about being someone else. That is a form of betrayal. You're supposed to be proud of who you are, Martin. So you try to stop dreaming, but you can't.

Elisabeth is staring out at the sunflowers. Mom is typing on her laptop. They are not talking. You notice them glancing at you as you read, then looking quickly back into the fields and the screen. Because you know them so well, you recognize their hope for you in their eyes.

# Thursday, May 19
## 6:00 p.m.

This morning, Elisabeth drove me to the *lycée* in the sky-blue Smart car. Mom said her production company had to buy it because Elisabeth is eighteen, and that's too young to drive a rental car in France. Elisabeth parked the Smart car on the street, then walked me down the sidewalk full of cigarette smoke outside the school, through the gate and the yard, to the office of the *directeur*, who said he was expecting me.

The outside of the *lycée* is concrete. The inside is white linoleum. There are bright-orange doors and orange metal staircases. I looked at my shoes all the way through the cracked yard and down the linoleum hallway. I kept looking at my shoes once we reached the office. They are black Converse slip-ons. They are decorated with silver moths, drawn in glitter pen by Layla.

Denim strings from my jeans were mixed up with Layla's moths.

The cuffs of my jeans are frayed. I'm very attached to these jeans. Elisabeth has patched the knees with soft gray corduroy. I was rubbing my soft knees while I stared at the Layla moths on my Converses.

"*Bienvenue, Martin*," the *directeur* said. He reached to shake my hand without forcing eye contact, which I appreciated. I lifted my right hand from my knee patch long enough to take his hand. Then I put it back. He said "Welcome" in English, with a thick French accent. His accent is much stronger than Papa's but not totally different. The *directeur* has a voice that I could get to know.

Elisabeth repeated what she'd already told me four times on the way down the hill to town. She said that whenever I felt done with my day I could text her to come get me. "You don't have to stay any longer than you want." She used her patient voice.

"Martin will be fine here," said the *directeur*. It was strange to hear another man besides Papa speak in

7

French. I was surprised I had no trouble understanding such a different voice.

The *directeur* was being optimistic. Mom says new people can be optimistic when they first see my chiseled features, my controlled manners, and my nice smile. Even if the nice smile is facing the floor. *Can it be that bad?* they wonder. Even though I am now six feet tall with a broken voice, Mom says my "elfin good looks" still make people want to help me. She tells me this is lucky.

The *directeur* led me down the hallway to a classroom and introduced me. The room was a soup of eyes and noses and teeth. It gagged me. My gaze skidded around for a place to land, a poster or a window blind or a scratch on a desktop. I needed something to hold on to so I wouldn't get swallowed up. Only I couldn't find it.

Standing in front of the class, I froze. What I saw grabbed my whole body and held it still. She was in the second-to-last row, but her image was right up in front of my face. I wondered if anyone else could see her.

She is what Marcel, who is the main character in *Search*, calls a *fillette*. She is a girl with strawberry-blond hair and freckles.

In class, she was holding a pen high up in the air, like she was making a point. I fell in love with her blue eyes, even though, from my reading of *Search*, I know they aren't in fact blue. I wanted to touch her all over, but I couldn't move. I was like a statue having a dream.

She was looking at me, holding back a smile. Unlike the other kids, she knew exactly who I was. She wanted to tease me, not because I'm different but because she was already familiar enough to tease. I sensed recognition but also tension. I wanted to impress her somehow, but all I could do was stare with stone eyes.

Her name is Gilberte. I know her from the book I call *Search*, although it has another title in the outside world. *Search* is a French novel from a hundred years ago, and it is also the story of my life right now. Seeing Gilberte come to life today was proof of everything I believe. Even though she was wearing modern clothes like me, we recognized each other from another time and place. Even if she didn't return my stare, she signaled me with her pen and her eyes. She signaled that I meant something to her.

"Have a seat," said the teacher. Here was another unfamiliar voice making sense in French. It was female and cracked. It went in the direction of a wooden chair with a desk table attached. The chair was in the front row. It was by a large window that looked out onto a basketball court.

Somehow, I unfroze and obeyed. I hated turning

away. Why hadn't I spoken up? Gilberte was so beautiful that I wanted to turn back and yell, "You're ugly!"

I wanted to grab her and pull her to me. Instead, I sat
with my back to her and tried to focus on red, blue, and
green words scrolling across a whiteboard at the front
of the room. My heart was pounding. I started to rock
back and forth to the pounding like I haven't rocked
since they taught me to stop. The legs of my chair were
hitting the floor in thuds.

"Perhaps you are not interested in the use of the sub-
junctive tense in Racine?" The teacher's shoes stopped
hard in front of my seat. They were black pumps with
ground-down heels. Her skirt hung to the middle of her
calves. It was gray. She smelled like tobacco.

"I don't know," I answered, loudly and clearly, in the
direction of my own feet. The French came flowing out.
I didn't have to think about it. "I don't know about that
because I have never read Racine. I do know that my favorite tense is the conditional."

"I'm afraid we are not here to learn what the American thinks."

There was laughter.

I rocked so hard I hit the desk behind me with the
back of my head. Then I stopped. I was sure I recognized

Gilberte's voice in the laughter. It was higher than the other voices. It was stormy. It had more spirit.

I stayed very still and listened. Even though this classroom was torture, I was grateful to be here. Because otherwise I might have missed her. It's a good thing I made it to school today.

I was supposed to come to the *lycée* yesterday, but I didn't. I told Mom that a school full of strangers would make me vomit. Instead, I wanted to go into town, stand outside the bakery window, and look at the madeleines. Mom said it was okay if I didn't go to school yet, but that I should give it a try soon because it wasn't appropriate for me to spend six weeks by myself wandering around a small French town.

Yesterday, I said, "I can't go. It will make me throw up."

"Okay," Mom said, looking up at the ceiling. The ceiling of our cottage is very low, with exposed beams and white plaster. Mom started breathing deeply, which is one of the ways she tricks herself into not being frustrated anymore. Finally she said, "Let's put it another way. Do you want to go to school today, or do you want to go tomorrow?"

There was only one possible answer. "Tomorrow. You want to go tomorrow. I mean, *I* want to go tomorrow."

"So you'll go tomorrow?"

"Yes, tomorrow. Not today. Today, I am going to the bakery."

"Okay," she said.

So I walked into town to stand outside the *boulangerie* and look at the madeleines through the window. The bakery is on a small green square with two plane trees and a wrought-iron bench.

A madeleine is a mini cake that has been molded in a scallop shell. It has ridges. It is yellow and buttery and spongy. When I finally do buy a madeleine, I'll take it back to the cottage. I'll dip it in my tea and eat it. I know exactly what will happen next. The taste will become the "immense edifice of memory" from the book I call *Search*. My life with Papa will come straight back to me.

When Marcel, who is the narrator of *Search*, tastes a madeleine dipped in tea, he remembers the taste from when he was a little boy spending the summer in the country. His country house was in a village called Combray. On his way to Sunday mass in Combray, he used to visit his sick old aunt Léonie. And she used to give him herbal tea with madeleines.

Years later, on a cold day, his mother tries to warm him up with the exact same snack. He almost doesn't take it because he's grumpy, but something makes him change his mind. When he swallows the madeleine, he's brought back to this moment with his aunt, and his whole past and everything he cares about comes back. When the tea mixed with the cake crumbs goes down his throat, all of Combray, from the flowers in his garden to the people of the village, rises up.

I started circling the bench facing the jingling bakery door. I circled it eleven times. I had this vision that I could breeze in and out of the shop, like any other customer. No need to look at the woman in pink behind the counter. Here in France, they don't know that there's anything weird about me. *Une madeleine, s'il vous plaît.* I wouldn't have to worry about my pronouns because there are none. It would all be cool.

But I couldn't go in. I wasn't ready to buy a madeleine yet. Because it wasn't a good idea to open that door alone. There was clearly someone I should wait for.

A dribbling basketball outside the open classroom window made a good thumping sound. The sound evened me out.

Thinking about how lucky I was to have found Gilberte in this class about Racine, I was able to stop rocking and sit quietly. I felt her eyes on my back.

The teacher didn't come close to me again. There was more writing on the whiteboard.

The bell rang. I jumped up, and my chair fell over sideways and clattered. The sea of students rose. Five smiles floated in my direction. It is impossible to return five smiles at once, so I did not try. I looked for Gilberte among the smiles, but she wasn't there.

She appears and then she vanishes. I have no proof that she isn't a ghost.

Suddenly, I felt exhausted. I needed to escape from this building full of strange kids. Out in the hallway, they seemed like ants rushing all over me. I had to get to a safe place where I could think about Gilberte. I buried my face in my phone and texted Elisabeth.

# Friday, May 20
## 5:15 p.m.

Since I only lasted an hour at school yesterday, they gave me a guide to help me through the day today. His name is Simon.

"*Ça va?*" Simon asked when the *directeur* introduced us in the yard. That means "How are you?" when you make it a question by raising your voice at the end. When you make it a statement, and not a question, it means "I'm fine." So when Simon asked "*Ça va?*" I could answer "*Ça va,*" then I could ask "*Ça va?*" back, and he could reply "*Oui, ça va.*" Then we could do the whole routine all over again. That's one of the good things about speaking French. You can keep batting "*Ça va*" back and forth with your partner while you let things settle.

Papa, who taught me French, used to play a game with me when I was little. The therapists at The Center gave him the idea, and he ran with it. We would ask "*Ça va?*" and answer "*Ça va*," over and over to each other, but we would have to change how we said it each time to give it a different meaning. The questions could be "Are you okay?" or "Are you even still alive?" or "Are you having fun?" And the answers could be "I'm bored," or "I'm fantastic," or "I'm going to puke"—but all with the same words: *Ça va*. You had to give them different meanings with your voice and your face. And you had to look the other person right in the eye while you were doing it. We got good at it. I even laughed. He did too. I don't know how much help the game has been to me, because there is no one besides Papa I could ever be so silly with. Not that Mom and Elisabeth aren't wonderful, but they aren't Papa. Mom and Elisabeth are everything to me now, but they are separate. They are not of my world.

Once Simon and I had done our *Ça va*s, he said we were going to math class and I said, "Math class. Thank you."

It was geometry, which I like.

When we came into the classroom, I scanned for

Gilberte. I could instantly see that she wasn't there. It was disappointing, but it also allowed me to relax a little.

Doing math in French instead of English isn't strange. The geometry proofs are the same. *Search* says that habit takes you in its arms.

In the hallway, walking from math class to history class, Simon asked when Baxter Wolff and Gloria Seegar are coming to start filming with Mom. I realized people here know I'm Samantha Mitchell's son, and they have been talking about her movie.

"Next week," I answered to his black Doc Martens. Forty percent of the shoes here are Doc Martens and twenty-five percent are Converses.

"Cool. Will you get to meet them?"

"As much as I meet anyone." This is a joke Papa taught me to make about myself. He said it would put people at ease.

Simon didn't get the joke. "What's the movie about?" he asked.

I repeated Mom's line: "It's a Renaissance costume drama. It's about the rivalry between two powerful women over the castle of Chenonceau during the reign of Henri II. One was the queen, Catherine de Médicis, and one was the king's mistress, Diane de Poitiers."

Simon took a few seconds to respond. I had given him

a lot of information. It may have sounded like I knew what I was talking about. But I don't know what I'm talking about. I'm an excellent parrot.

Elisabeth is the one who understands Mom's movies. I don't like them until I've seen them at least ten times with Layla on the couch in her basement. And I certainly never understand them before they exist.

When Simon finally reacted, he said, "*Sympa*," which is short for *sympathique*. It means a combination of "nice" and "cool."

Then he said, "Maybe you will tell us where the actors are staying and if there is any love between them?" He laughed. "Maybe you will even invite us to a party where they will be?"

I took a quick glance up from his shoes toward his face. I saw pointed eyebrows, an upturned nose, and high cheekbones. He is Bloch from *Search*.

Bloch is Marcel's intellectual friend. He gives Marcel books by a writer named Bergotte. Marcel goes crazy for Bergotte's writing. One day Marcel's brilliant neighbor, Mr. Charles Swann, sees Marcel reading a Bergotte novel under a tree, and asks where he got it. Marcel answers that the book is a present from his friend Bloch. It turns out Mr. Swann is friends with Bloch too. Mr. Swann describes Bloch's pointed eyebrows, upturned nose, and high cheekbones. He says they are exactly like a portrait of Mahomet II by Bellini. "Once he grows a goatee, he will be the same person," says Mr. Swann.

One of the reasons I love Mr. Swann is that he recognizes people through pictures he studies and loves. Matching up people with pictures makes perfect sense to me.

Simon looks like Bloch, who looks like Mahomet II. This made me want to be his friend. But I wasn't ready.

Walking down the hallway past all the bright-orange doors, I got anxious. I wanted to text Elisabeth to come rescue me. But I'd promised her I would do everything I could to at least make it through lunch today. So instead I texted Layla, even though it was the middle of the night back home. Mom has given me an unlimited texting plan. I am much more skilled at writing than at talking out loud.

**I'm spending the morning with a moth named Simon.**

Layla wrote back immediately, **Is he a colorful moth or a gray one?**

**Maybe colorful. He is exactly like Bloch, from *Search*. What are you doing up so late?**

**I'm watching Matthew's accident.**

Matthew was a character in *Downton Abbey* until he

was killed off the show in a car accident. He was married to Lady Mary. She is the oldest, the most glamorous, of the three *Downton* sisters. Matthew had a World War I wound that seemed like it would leave him paralyzed. Only it didn't. He recovered, got married, had a baby, and then he died in a stupid car accident. The final shot of the last episode of Season Three shows Matthew's lifeless, bleeding face on the side of the road. This is one of the episodes Layla has gotten me to watch a few times. Layla has watched it over one hundred times. She says that in every repetition she sees something new in Matthew's dead eyes.

I didn't answer Layla right away because Simon was asking me if I had met Peter Bird when he starred in Mom's Sherlock Holmes movie. It took all my politeness to say, "Yes, but I'm not sure what he's like."

"How come you speak French so well?" asked another boy walking next to Simon.

I'm used to being taken for a freaky genius with mental superpowers, like the ability to learn whole languages in a few days. For all these kids know, I might have mastered French last week. But I don't have what they call "savant syndrome." The only thing unique about me is my own bubble that I mostly live in. I'm good at math and I have a good memory for certain details, but nothing special. I can't surprise people, seconds after they tell me their birth date, with the fact that they were born on a rainy Tuesday or a sunny Sunday. I'm not cool that way. That's not me.

When I didn't answer him, the boy in the hallway, blue Converse high-tops, tried again. "It's crazy for an American to speak French like this, no?"

"My dad is French," I blurted.

"*Sympa*," said Simon. "Is your dad here too?"

"No, he's back in the States." This is true.

"He has to work in America?" Simon asked.

"Sort of," I said. I didn't feel like explaining to Simon about Papa.

Now I really wanted to text Elisabeth to get me out of here, because things were starting to move too fast. "Come on. Just make it through lunch," I said to myself, out loud, in English. The scuffed white of the hallway floor filled my eyes.

"What's on your shoes?" blue-Converse boy asked me.

"Oh, those are moths that a friend of mine drew."

There was a silence, and then Simon said, "*Sympa*."

I was grateful.

We arrived at history class.

**Gotta go**, I texted Layla, with a tearful emoji to show that I wasn't ignoring the sadness of her dead-Matthew episode.

After history, I tried lunch. The cafeteria was hard. Gilberte wasn't there. In the food line, I recognized a slice of familiar cake called a "quatre-quarts," which means "four quarters" because it has four ingredients: butter, flour, sugar, and eggs. It's almost the same as pound cake. It was the only thing I felt like eating. I took a slice and went to sit down at a table with Simon.

"Is that all you're having?" asked Simon.

"I like quatre-quarts," I said. I forced myself to look at his plate of hot food and then up at his face. It was definitely the portrait of Mahomet II by Bellini. I have a postcard of it in my collection.

"I like quatre-quarts too," said Simon. I recognized his words as an example of friendliness, a way to find common ground. "They remind me of when I was a kid and life was easy." Then he changed the subject to Gloria Seegar. He asked if I knew what she likes to eat.

"She likes sashimi and avocados with lime juice," I said.

I was burning to ask Simon if he happened to be friends with a beautiful strawberry-blond girl named Gilberte. Then a wave of people crashed all around us with trays and teenage slang that I mostly didn't get since I learned my French first as a young kid and then from an old novel. All I had to hold on to was my cake. I took tiny bites because I had to make it last through the lunch period or I might go under.

"*Ça va?*" Simon asked.

"*Ça va.*" I made a lame smile into space and kept up my super-slow chewing.

The cake reminded me of being a kid too. Papa and I used to bake quatre-quarts together all the time. We were supposed to branch out and bake many different kinds of cakes. But after a few disasters trying to vary our routine, we stopped pretending.

When I was six, a speech therapist told Papa that my thoughts were like the ingredients of a cake. I could line them up beautifully, one next to the other on the kitchen counter, measured, counted, and repeated, but I couldn't mix them together to create something new.

Papa refused to believe I would never be more than a list of ingredients. And so we started baking cakes together. They were delicious, golden, and buttery. The whole family loved them at first, and Papa and I loved them unconditionally. We baked almost every day.

Mom started to get annoyed that the kitchen was always dusted in flour and the mixing bowls were sticky.

Once she yelled at Papa, "Is this really what you quit your job to do?!" And he yelled back, "This *is* my goddamn job!" Then he smashed an egg on the floor, which Mom said was a pathetic gesture. She said the cake baking was a kind of voodoo superstition, but then she took me aside and said she didn't mean it.

I wiped up the egg with a dishrag. I enjoy the circular movement of a rag.

I miss Papa's and my quatre-quarts. I miss the measuring, the pouring, and the stirring, but mostly the way they tasted. So much better than this cafeteria version.

The other kids in the cafeteria were glancing at my tiny bites, but I didn't make them any bigger. I made the cake last all the way through lunch.

# Saturday, May 21
## 11:30 a.m.

Mom was excited about the croissants she bought at the *boulangerie* this morning. She said they were "flaky and fresh," that they "managed to make butter seem airy." She squinted while she ate hers. The sun shone on her hair, which is long, thick, and wavy, light brown with a few gray streaks. The sun made the gray streaks silver.

We ate the croissants on our stone terrace in the sunshine. Mom was smiling, but not her tight smile that makes her cheekbones pop out, not her smile for when she is working hard to get people to do what they need to do. This was her other smile, where her teeth show and the skin wrinkles around her eyes. This is the smile that relaxes me. I tried to smile back at her with the same soft lips and crinkly eyes. I like it when we are similar.

The cottage we've rented is on a hill. It is made of uneven, sand-colored stones. It has two chimneys. It has four windows in front, four in back, and two on each side. The shutters are painted red. There is ivy growing halfway up the façade. There is a big lilac bush with white flowers by the door, which is red like the shutters. At the front of the cottage is a terrace with a green downward-sloping view to a river. I call the river the Vivonne because that's the name of the river that Marcel follows on his afternoon walks.

Today at breakfast, an actress named Fuchsia came over. Fuchsia has large, distracting breasts. She said she didn't eat flour or butter but she would eat our croissants because they looked "special." This made no sense to me, but I have learned that most of the people Mom works with are inconsistent. They are different things to different people at different times, like many of the characters in *Search*. And this is how I'm able to understand them, by knowing I can't.

Mom also brought some local jams: rhubarb, apricot, and green plum.

"Rhubarb is my favorite!" I said.

"Martin," said Mom, "rhubarb is *my* favorite. Now, can you tell me what *your* favorite is?" Her smile went away and her forehead furrowed into lines. Mom worries a lot about my pronouns.

Until I was eight years old, I called myself "you" because that's what everyone else called me, and I called other people "I" because that's what they called themselves. Once I finally learned to read, I was mostly able to get it straight. But still, I can't say pronouns right when I'm nervous, and Fuchsia was making me nervous.

"I don't know," I said. And then it came out again, in a perfect echo: "Rhubarb is *my* favorite. Now, Martin, can you tell me what *your* favorite is?"

Mom looked away.

"I sense a teaching moment, Martin," Elisabeth said. I didn't understand why the teaching-moment thing was funny in this situation, but I could tell it was supposed to be funny from her joking tone, and so I laughed.

"Let's do a blind taste test," she said. "Close your eyes."

I closed my eyes. I was happy to be getting her attention. Even when I can't see Elisabeth in real life, I can see her perfectly in my head. She has gray eyes, like Papa's and mine, and pale skin but almost no freckles, and a very high forehead with a widow's peak. She has a thin, pointy face. Her hair is redder than Mom's. It would fall down past her shoulders if she didn't pull it back into a ponytail.

Because her hair was up, I could see her ears. They were golden at the edges where the sun touched them. She was wearing a royal-blue bathrobe. She looked like a holy figure from one of the medieval paintings in my collection. Mr. Swann loved medieval paintings.

With my eyes still closed, I heard Fuchsia talking. "The geraniums in these pots are such a marvelous color. What gorgeous stone pots," she said. "Did all these Provençal dishes come with the rental? These bowls with the ear-shaped handles on either side are fantastic. They call them elephant ears." She tried to pronounce "elephant ears" in French—"*oreilles d'éléphant*"—but it sounded so out of tune that I winced.

Three spoonfuls of jam came into my mouth, one after the other.

"Keep your eyes closed," said Elisabeth. "Don't cheat. Concentrate on the flavor. Is it sweet? A bit sour maybe? And the texture. Are there strings, berries, flecks of fruit? Which one do *you* prefer?"

The first two were very sweet and unfamiliar. I didn't like them. The last spoonful I recognized. It expanded inside me into a giant memory of Papa. He loved this taste too. Our old kitchen sprung up behind my closed eyes. We were sitting there at the breakfast table, with crumbs and jam smears on our plates. We were back together having toast with butter and jam. He was touching a light-yellow napkin to his chin, which was dark from stubble because he was working from home. I was thirteen. He was handing me the first volume of *Search*, *Swann's Way*. It was a Folio Classique paperback with a picture of a little boy in a blue-and-white-striped shirt and navy sailor jacket. In French, the title is *Du côté de chez Swann*. The boy on the book has dark hair and gray eyes, like Papa and me.

Papa said, "This is the first volume of *In Search of Lost Time* by Marcel Proust." His voice was deep and a little shaky, like a lake in a breeze. He was speaking softly, even though there was no one in the house to be quiet for since there were only the two of us. "Between us, let's call it *Search*. In my opinion, it's the greatest book ever written. It says the most about life, the most about pain, and the most about the way our minds can make us happy."

Two years later he was gone. I miss him more than anything.

I opened my eyes and made the effort to say, "Elisabeth, I prefer the third jam."

"You see, Mom." Elisabeth laughed. "He *does* prefer

the rhubarb after all. You don't have a monopoly on it. Martin has his own mind. Give him some credit!"

"Yay, Martin!" Fuchsia chimed in.

Fuchsia is not a total stranger because I have watched her seven times in Mom's movie about Henry VIII. She hovers on the skin of my bubble. I can see her, but not for very long.

I remembered from the movie that she was pretty with sparkly blue eyes and those big breasts. I knew I should look at her, since she had congratulated me. I tried for her face, but ended up staring at her chest instead. The breasts were confusing now in a white T-shirt instead of squished forward and laced up in period costume, but they were recognizable.

Fuchsia does not drink coffee, so she was having a verveine infusion with breakfast. I wished I could smile up at her blue eyes, but it wasn't happening. Instead, I forced myself to shift focus from her breasts to her herbal tea. At first, this wasn't easy. Then I got interested in watching the dead leaves. They were expanding in the boiling water as though they were coming back to life. "Those leaves of yours are embalmed spring evenings," I said. I was quoting Marcel.

"Wow," she said to Mom, "you did tell me he was special. He sure is!"

*Special* is one of the words I have no picture for. It doesn't attach to anything in my mind. People call me "special" a lot, and I can't understand it. When I hear "special," I see blobs.

I stopped worrying about Fuchsia. I put rhubarb jam on my croissant and winked across time at Papa.

## 10:15 p.m.

This afternoon, I felt Gilberte's eyes on my back, and I whipped around to look for her.

I was wandering through the hawthorn bushes down the road from our cottage, listening to Vinteuil's sonata, when her gaze landed. I turned, but there were only the white flowers with white spray in their centers. Thousands of white flowers and no girl.

When I couldn't see her, I even took my headphones off in the middle of the second movement so that I could hear her if she crunched the ground running away. I hate interrupting my music. It hurts. So there was something very important going on to make me do it.

I took off my headphones and let my brain rip as the music pulled away from it. I had to suffer to give myself the chance to hear her footsteps or to catch sight of her face. In her own strange way, she was saying hello, and

I had to show her that I was paying attention. I started pushing branches aside, like I could somehow rustle her up if I made enough commotion. I had to meet her.

Only I didn't meet her.

I met Elisabeth, who usually makes me happy, but not this time, because she was not Gilberte. Elisabeth came walking up to me in the hawthorns, holding her giant chemistry book with the blue molecule on the cover. Her ponytail was looser and lower than usual, so that her free hair made a pretty red-gold spray around her face. I noticed that her arms, neck, and legs were less pale than usual. They are turning a dusty gold, probably because she is doing most of her work on the terrace or by the pool.

Elisabeth was wearing her red dress, which I have seen eight times and have grown to love. She sewed it herself. It has little white flowers shaped the same as the blossoms on the hawthorn bushes. She saw me looking from the blossoms on her dress to the real live ones on the bushes and back. I liked the repetition of the patterns.

"Can you tell I'm trying to blend into the landscape with my flowery dress?" She smiled. She smiles a lot, and when she does, her upper lip pulls way up to show her gums. She says she can't help it. She's a mostly happy person even though she has a brother who is fixated on a hundred-year-old French novel and repeats a lot of what she says back to her. "You, of all people, should appreciate my effort to celebrate the flowers," she said.

"Celebrate the flowers," I repeated, because it sounded so nice.

Elisabeth is very smart. She's becoming a psychiatrist, like Maeva. She finished high school a whole semester early so that she could come on location with Mom and me before she does her summer internship in a hospital and then goes to college at Stanford. After Stanford, she will go to medical school. I don't want her to leave us, and that's one of the reasons she has come to France: to say good-bye to me.

I did not finish my year at The Center early. I am following along with my classwork from here, emailing assignments. The Center is still my school. It's a very small school for kids with challenges. I've been there since kindergarten. Mom is very involved and helps with fundraising by inviting all of her famous friends to the annual benefit. Papa used to be involved too. He used to volunteer every Tuesday and Thursday morning in the library.

The *lycée* in Chenonceaux is not my real school. It is the place I go to practice French and perhaps to make some friends. I could never actually do the work there. I'm not general-ed enough.

In the bushes today, Elisabeth told me, "You're lucky you have your bubble because you can keep me inside, close to you all the time. I'm not going anywhere!"

She thinks she's kidding when she says that she's not leaving. What she doesn't realize is that she's not kidding. Not at all. Because I do have a super-strong bubble, and she's not going anywhere outside it, not to Stanford, not to medical school, not anywhere.

"Are you coming back to the house?" she asked. "Want to walk together?"

"Thank you, but I don't want to walk together," I said. "I need to wait a little longer."

"Wait for what?"

"Wait for what? Just wait."

"Okay." She smiled again.

I wanted my music back. I started fiddling with my headphones.

"Let me guess what you're listening to."

"Let me guess? Let you guess?" This word order always confuses me.

"I know what you're listening to, silly. I'm teasing you, but not in a mean way, okay?" She thinks it's a good idea

34

to tease me gently so that I will learn about humor as a way to interact. It's very kind of her. "Don't look so sad. It's a pretty sonata. It's fine."

It's a pretty violin-and-piano sonata by a composer named César Franck. In *Search*, Proust changed it into the *Sonate de Vinteuil*. I find it crazy beautiful. Only I've learned that if I don't control myself and I play it over and over, they will take my music away, because too much music keeps me outside reality. So I keep my listening under control.

My music fixation is as old as I am. Sixteen.

Before my parents put me in The Center, when I was in a regular preschool, I started to freak out about music. Whenever the teachers, or Mom or Papa, stopped playing a CD of my nursery songs before it was finished, or if they skipped a song or repeated one so that the order changed, I started to scream. Not an angry scream but a painful one. At first, they all thought I was super smart because I knew all these songs by heart, in French and in English, and because I seemed to care so much about them that it literally hurt to take them away.

Mom and Papa went from being delighted that I could sing so well to being very scared.

I remember hearing Mom through the bedroom wall

when I was five. She was crying. "He's Rain Man," she sobbed. "We thought he was so cute, and he's actually Rain Man. How could we be so blind?"

"He's still cute," whispered Papa, who knew I was listening, because I loved to listen to their voices while I fell asleep. Their voices were the next best thing to music. "He's still wonderful."

"Of course he is," Mom tried to whisper too, but she was still screeching. "But it's not what we assumed. It's nothing like what we assumed."

"No, it's not. It's a surprise. It's a turn ' . . . *je tourne une rue . . . mais . . . c'est dans mon coeur.'*"

"What does that mean?" Mom doesn't speak much French.

"It's from Proust, about losing your way and wanting to ask directions, making a turn, realizing the turn you have made is not on the street but within your heart, and it is about to take you back to yourself."

"Can you just speak English? This is important."

Suddenly, I echoed loudly from my bed through the wall. "Can you just speak English? This is important." I took a breath and kept going. "'. . . *je tourne une rue . . . mais . . . c'est dans mon coeur.'* What does that mean? What does that mean? What does that mean?" I yelled.

Mom and Papa were silent.

"He's still cute!" I cried out. "How could we be so blind?"

When I was older, I found Papa's sentence in *Search*. ". . . *je tourne une rue . . . mais . . . c'est dans mon coeur.*" Marcel is talking about the bell tower in Combray, which made a huge impression on him when he was a boy, and how sometimes as an adult wandering in a new city, asking directions to get where he needs to go, he'll stumble on a bell tower, and he'll just stare at it. He'll forget the actual turn he was supposed to make in whatever town he's in. That's when he realizes the turn he's taking is inside himself, and not on any map.

I watched Elisabeth go, and I stayed, pacing through the hawthorns, thrusting the branches aside as though I might uncover Gilberte. Even though the tug was strong, I didn't put my headphones back on. Maeva would be proud of me for not retreating into my music.

In case she was still watching, I showed Gilberte that I don't give up easily.

Gilberte is the proud daughter of Mr. Charles Swann. The Swanns have an estate near Marcel's summer house in Combray.

Mr. Swann is the perfect neighbor. He charms everybody in Marcel's family. He knows all about art and literature. He always shows up with beautiful presents. But

Marcel's family never goes to Mr. Swann's because Mrs. Swann is the "wrong kind" of woman. Her name used to be Odette de Crécy, and she was a "high-class prostitute" before she married Mr. Swann. Marcel isn't allowed to see Odette or her daughter, Gilberte. The Swann estate is off-limits.

The idea of the forbidden Gilberte grips Marcel. Mr. Swann talks a lot about his daughter. He tells Marcel that she's friends with famous writers and painters. She seems like a myth. The first time Marcel sees her, it happens by accident during a country walk with his father and grandfather. She is going through the hawthorns holding up a gardening shovel. He stares at her, the taboo strawberry-blond girl from Mr. Swann's art world. He stares until he is yanked away by the adults. Marcel is so frustrated that he wishes he had been brave enough to yell some insult at her. He should have told her she was ugly, which is the opposite of the truth. Anything to make her notice and remember him.

I feel the same. I should have yelled something into those bushes. But I'm not very good on the spot.

# Sunday, May 22
## 8:45 p.m.

My room is in the cottage's attic, so it has sloping walls. It's a small space, which I like because it contains me. It has light-blue wallpaper between exposed beams. The beams run up and down the walls and along the line of the ceiling where the two walls meet. The room is a tent framed by old wood.

Swinging from one of the beams above my narrow bed are two cobwebs that I have grown friendly with.

There is a window by my bed that I leave open a crack at night. I don't pull down the shades because I like the geraniums in my window box. The crickets sing very loudly. At first, their song was a back-and-forth seesaw in my gut. I had to put my headphones on to block the crickets out. But two nights ago their music started rocking me gently instead of making me seasick.

This evening, I Skyped Maeva's Sunday-morning life-skills group with other kids from The Center. It's nine hours earlier in Los Angeles. The kids were eating pancakes. Some were eating blueberry pancakes and some chocolate-chip pancakes. Maeva was eating oatmeal and drinking coffee.

Layla was there. Her pancakes were blueberry, as always. Layla is very small for her age, which is sixteen, like mine. But on my laptop, she appeared very big. She has dark hair and green eyes with black lashes that are often clumped together in groups of two or three. She clumps them on purpose with her mascara, to be distinctive. On-screen they looked especially dark and matted, like a close-up of spider legs. And her hands around her blue mug of mint tea looked even more enormous and out of proportion to her body than they are in real life. She can stretch them to play octaves on the piano.

The group was sitting in their usual booth at the Honest Bean Cafe on Beverly Boulevard in West Hollywood.

It's Maeva's favorite place. We've all been meeting with her at the Honest Bean since sixth grade. The booth up-holstery is dark red. There is a large framed poster of an ice-cream sundae at eye level. Seeing the cherry on top of the sundae made me feel at home. Then I noticed a tiny bright patch on the cherry, a reflection of light. I had never seen this reflection before. Noticing the bright patch made me feel slightly different from the Martin who used to sit under that poster, back at home, before I came to France.

Maeva, who has blond hair and a muscular body, was wearing black like she always does. The way the layers of her clothes all flowed into one another was very famil-iar and comforting. But then I noticed that she had cut her hair from very long to shoulder length, and I felt dif-ferent again.

"Hi, Martin." Maeva smiled at me. "How are you doing? How's France?"

I looked at Maeva, Layla, Joey, Claire, and Mitchell on-screen with their pancake plates, syrup jugs, mugs, and glasses of orange juice. I took a deep breath and said, "I feel that France is the beginning of my real life."

"That's fantastic," said Maeva. "Can you explain why?"

Before I could answer, Mitchell interrupted. "Is it because you're in a general-ed school? Layla told us

41

you're in a general-ed school. Is that true? Is that really the case?"

"Yes," I answered, "that is the case. But that's not why my life is starting for real. What I mean is that certain things are going to happen to me in France because I've read them in *Search*. Actually, things are already starting to happen."

Next Layla chimed in her support. "Martin, you are destined to be in France right now just like Lady Grantham was destined to move to England to save Downton Abbey with her American fortune."

"Thanks, Layla," I said.

"Can you tell us one of the things that has happened to you so far?" asked Maeva.

"Well, I've met a strawberry-blond girl with freckles named Gilberte Swann, who is my love interest."

"Where did you meet her?"

"Well, I haven't exactly met her yet, but I've seen her. That's what's supposed to happen first. I see her and think a lot about her, and then I meet her and then we eventually get close."

"Martin, is this girl really called Gilberte Swann or does she remind you strongly of the character?" Maeva asked.

This question made me uncomfortable. I stared at the

kids in the Honest Bean Cafe. They stared back. Finally, I mumbled, "She reminds me strongly." I knew this had to be the right answer. But it was not the answer I wanted.

"I need to say something!" Layla was suddenly yelling. Her eyes got wide and jittery. They looked like pinwheels. She slammed her mug down, and her tea sprayed out onto the table. "I want you to know that your affinity is getting in the way right now."

Layla has warned me before that, even though she supports me, it can seem pretentious for a boy my age to talk so much about a twentieth-century French novel. She points out that I don't even know what half the words in the book mean. She also understands, because we are similar in certain ways, that I would much rather be comfortable with my book than cool without it.

So why is she giving me a hard time? She knows better. Force of habit makes me carry *Search* around, because it has filled me up like an empty glass for years. This force is so strong that it's hard to care about anything else, like everyone thinking I'm weird. Everyone thinking I'm weird has become habit too.

Layla and I are both attached to stories. I like Proust, and she likes *Downton Abbey*. Other Center kids are way into movies. Joey first learned to talk using Disney animation.

Kids like us watch our shows and imitate what we see and hear. We do this until it all starts to connect with something inside of us. Then we can start to express ourselves. First, we do it in echoes. Then we move on to what they call "variations." It's a kind of backward learning. It teaches us how to act. At The Center, they've given us a name to this backwardness. They call it "affinity." They say "affinity therapy" can help us to break through to the outside.

With a book, there's less to imitate than with movies or TV. There are only the words to go on, no images. So my brain has to work extra hard. I have to picture Marcel and Mr. Swann for myself. Layla's *Downton Abbey* is full of visuals, like faces with expressions. She says I've made a hard choice.

She also understands that I didn't choose *Search*. It chose me. You might say I walk around in a prison. But at least it's a prison that moves, not some cage stuck in one spot. I'm surrounded by *Search* the way most people are surrounded by their own souls.

"Layla," Maeva asked with a gentle voice. "When you say Martin's affinity for his book is getting in the way, what do you mean? Getting in the way of what?"

"Just getting in the way!" Layla's voice was too loud.

She banged her mug again. Then she closed her eyes tightly while we all watched, and she did what Maeva calls "rechanneling." When she opened her eyes, she changed the subject. " 'A lack of compassion can be as vulgar as an excess of tears.' "

"Are you quoting your show?" asked Mitchell.

"Yes. Lady Grantham said that." Layla smiled, and I felt relieved.

"Maybe this relates to what Mitchell was saying the other day about how affinities are a portal into real life," Maeva said. "Does anyone have any more thoughts about this or about Martin's book now that he is actually in France?"

Instead of answering her, everyone started to talk about their shows. I said I should probably get going. So we all high-fived and fist-bumped. I noticed as I rapped on the screen that I missed the feeling of real hands. Then we said good-bye. The cherry on the sundae poster was the last thing to vanish when I switched off the group.

I'm the only kid at The Center who likes to be affectionate. Once I get to know people, that is. I enjoy the touch of familiar skin. It holds me like water. So it's been hard for me to understand that most of my friends don't like to be touched or hugged. Even Layla won't get closer than a fist bump. Her fist is tight and her knuckles are very white.

Twenty minutes after I turned off my Skype, Layla texted me. **It was good to see you. The brown couch in your French house looks comfortable. How's the movie? How are the moths? Do you think our phones are instruments of communication or torture?**

When she is in a philosophical mood, Layla signs off her messages with: **Do you think our phones are instruments of communication or torture?** This is her version of a quote from Lady Grantham, played by Maggie Smith. Mom has promised to introduce Layla to Maggie Smith someday, because Mom has good access to famous people. Layla reminds Mom of this promise every time she sees her.

Layla is interested in the star-studded aspect of Mom's movies. She's attracted to the idea of glamour. This is because a television show has taught her how to be.

*Downton Abbey* would not interest me at all if it didn't remind me of Layla. I have only watched three episodes, including Matthew's accident, in her basement. So most of her quoting sounds original to me. She says the same about mine, because she hasn't read *Search*.

Layla makes a point of asking questions in her texts.

The Center teaches us that questions are important. They are a good strategy for conversations. A person should show an interest in details, even if the interest is fake. If she acts curious enough, eventually the pretend interest will become real. Layla has reached this point in her questioning where she cares about the answers.

I answered her text right away. **Mom's movie is starting to shoot. Fuchsia is here. The big stars come next week. The moths aren't around yet.**

**All good**, she answered. When she writes very short texts, it means she is watching an episode and can't focus, but she still wants to send at least a couple of words so that she doesn't leave me hanging.

I sent her back a smiling emoji. Emojis are an autistic kid's dream.

# Monday, May 23
## 3:30 p.m.

Today, Simon got angry at me. We were going down one of the two orange staircases between the second and third floor of the school building. I was watching his black heels land on the steps in front of me. I blurted out, "Do you know a girl with reddish blond hair in our class?"

He stopped walking and turned around. "What's her name?" he asked.

"It might be Gilberte," I said hopefully.

He shook his head. "Any other ideas?"

I shook my head.

"Listen," he said with a darkness in his voice. "I have

to go visit my dad today, so I can't be with you this afternoon, but my friend Marianne said she could hang out if you want."

"Where's your dad?"

"In jail." He laughed and looked down at his shoes.

"So is mine." I did not laugh. One of the things they teach us at The Center is to point out similarities between our experiences and other people's. It's a good social skill. It can also make us less lonely.

"Fuck you, idiot! I was kidding, okay?" He ran ahead of me down the steps.

I was too upset to focus on what I might have done wrong. I felt sliced up inside. I sat down and put my head between my knees in the recovery position Maeva taught me. I counted twenty breaths.

While I was counting, the bell rang for the start of my next class, which was history. When I looked up, the staircase was empty.

I did not go to history class. I walked all the way home.

## 11:30 p.m.

"How was school?" Mom asked this softly. We were eating tonight in a restaurant called La Poule. "Were you more comfortable?" She hopes I'll be able to hide the fact that I don't always communicate by acting "attentive" in class. She also hopes the way I look will help the other kids accept me.

I told her this week was not starting out well.

"Give it a few more days. If you end up miserable, you don't have to go back. But it might be a nice way for you to meet some local kids. You're lucky you can speak French so fluently. Most people wouldn't have this chance."

She sat down across from me at a long, narrow table, which was filling up with her cast and crew. There was a red-and-white-checked cloth on the table; candles in glass jars; plates decorated with chickens, roosters, and cows; and pitchers of red wine. The ceiling was low. Three small windows set in thick walls let in light. The light struck the four copper pots decorating the wall that faced me. On a buffet below the pots was a tarte Tatin, only it was made with apricots instead of apples.

Someone offered me rillettes, which is my favorite pâté.

"*Oui, s'il vous plaît, je voudrais des rillettes.*"

"*Vous parlez français?*" It was a woman's voice.

"*Oui.*"

She asked if I liked rillettes, and I answered "*Oui*" again.

How had this happened that I spoke French, the woman wanted to know.

"My father taught me," I said.

"No," Mom interrupted, "you speak French because you yourself learned."

She never wants to give Papa credit for anything.

Elisabeth sits down next to me. Because there are so many blurry new faces in the group, I focus on her clear profile. She has a small nose that turns up at the tip. Her eyebrow looks very arched and reddish gold in the candlelight. Her eye is bright. Her hair is in a loose bun. There are two small moles on her chin that I can see from my angle. And there is one more that I can't see now.

On the other side of Elisabeth sits a man with a brown beard. She is talking to the man very fast, in a squeakier voice than usual. Everything about her face while she talks is precise, while the man next to her is a mass of fur on top of a black T-shirt with some kind of design on it, maybe even some words.

The mass of fur stands up and says he will be right back.

Elisabeth now turns to face me so that I see both shiny eyes and both eyebrows and the point of her widow's peak marking the middle of her pretty face. I also see her collarbones and part of her chest because she is wearing her white cotton shirt with the top four buttons undone.

"What do you think of Arthur?"

"Is Arthur the man who is hairy, with some light brown and some dark brown?"

"You don't like his beard?"

"I don't know. I've never seen him before. I have an impression of furriness."

She laughs.

"Well, he's great. He's the art director for the movie. He's smart and he speaks French, like you. You should talk to him."

This is not an appealing idea at all. I tell her she can talk to him instead and tell me about it later.

She says okay.

Soon the hairy art director named Arthur comes back and Elisabeth goes into profile and starts to squeak again. Then some asparagus vinaigrette comes and I am served five spears. I focus all my attention on them. They are delicious. The taste helps to block out the noise of conversations.

"More asparagus, please?" I say, lifting my voice to make it sound like a question instead of an order.

I can clearly see Mom's lips across the table, starting to form the full question for me to repeat and learn.

This is the question she wants to model for me: "May I have some more asparagus, please?" She wants to help me because there are a lot of strangers with us at the table, and I'm trying to avoid saying "I" in case I say "you" by mistake, as in "You want more asparagus, please?"

Mom holds back because she doesn't want to make a big deal in front of everyone. After she mouths the first two words, "May I . . ." she clamps her mouth shut into her tight-cheekbone smile. She badly wants me to fit in because she believes it's important to *me* to fit in. This is called "projection."

Layla says that neurotypical people project on us a lot. They think we can be happy only if we become like them. They don't understand that the way we are is the only way we can be, like having blue eyes, or being male or female, or being human even. It's not something we can change, Layla says, and they should stop making us try. I'm not sure what my own opinion about this is, but I think about it more than once every day.

Someone hands me the plate of asparagus. I take it, ducking the hander's gaze.

"Thank you," I say to the plate, taking only five more spears because I have learned from Françoise, the family cook in *Search*, how much trouble they are to prepare.

53

"Do you want some of this frothy sauce?" asks a large man whose voice is not totally foreign. He must have worked on some of Mom's other movies. He's sitting to the right of her, across the table.

I half raise my eyes, and I see that he has a wisp of a beard, less dense than the art director's. I can't make out his other features. Compared to Mom, he is broad-shouldered and massive. His shirt is solid gray.

On the left side of Mom is another large man, but this one is rounder and his skin is smooth and very white. His hair is a splash of yellow. His shirt is a splash of light blue mixed with green.

Mom is a focused image in between two blurred ones. The brown-and-gray curves of her hair are like sculpture. Her eyes are round, and her lower lashes are almost as thick as her top lashes, so that they look like the sunflower petals from the fields in the country-side around here. She is wearing her pale gray dress with the black beading. She is also wearing two silver pendants on thick chains. The pendants are cameos of my face and of Elisabeth's face from when we were babies. When I stare at my baby profile around Mom's neck, I realize that when Papa had it made for her she still had no idea that there was anything wrong with me. This makes it a relic.

While I am staring at the pendant on the skin of Mom's neck, which is sunburned, the voice of the man to the right repeats its question: "Hey, do you want some of this frothy sauce?"

*"Sauce mousseline!"* I yell, trying to look at him, but seeing a gleaming pot on the wall behind him instead.

The man laughs and asks me if I read a lot of cookbooks.

I say, "Yes, I read them from cover to cover."

Here is a list of my six favorite recipes: quatre-quarts cake, ratatouille, cassoulet, chocolate mousse, leg of lamb with mustard, couscous.

# Tuesday, May 24
## 10:20 a.m.

Elisabeth came into my room. She was wearing her long, soft white T-shirt with the word COFFEE spelled in block letters across the front. This is her favorite thing to sleep in.

She sat on the edge of my bed. She told me she drank too much wine last night and had a headache. I said I was sorry. Then she asked me if I thought Arthur seemed too old for her.

I asked her what she meant.

She answered, "Mom says I'm too young to date him, but I think it's more that she's weirded out that I would be with somebody who is from her world."

"What about Jason?" I asked. "Maybe Mom is worried about Jason."

Jason is Elisabeth's boyfriend who is a sophomore at UCLA film school. Even though he has been in the picture for two years, I do not like to look at him. He has a hiss in his voice that scares me. And his arms snake around Elisabeth in a way that makes me picture boa constrictors. The arms and the hiss stop me from wanting to know Jason. He can tell. He doesn't talk to me much.

"Jason is bugging me," she said, looking at her feet. Her toenails are painted sky blue. She sounded sad though, not like someone was bugging her. But I didn't want to contradict her. So instead I explained a fact from *Search*. "Sometimes," I said, "you meet someone new, like Arthur, and they erase everything that has gone before."

"You're a trip." She laughed. Then she stretched and said she wanted to go dive in the pool to clear her head. She asked me why I'm ditching school. "Did Mom give you a hard time?"

I said I did not want to talk about it, and that Mom was cool. Then she asked what I was doing today.

I said I was going to hang out on set for a while. "I'm going to watch Fuchsia in a high-ruffled collar strolling through the palace gardens while Mom tells everyone around her what to do."

When I told Elisabeth my plan, she squinted at me. She squints like Mom, only the wrinkles around her eyes smooth out right away when she is done, unlike Mom's, which stay for a while. When Elisabeth squints, it is a sign that she is joking around. "I'm on to you," Elisabeth said.

She told me that between Fuchsia's collar and the top of her dress there will be transparent lace so her cleavage will be very visible. "But you should know they aren't real," she said. Then she left.

I'm wondering how Fuchsia's breasts can not be real when they are so real in my mind. I'm also wondering how it is that I can picture Gilberte's breasts so clearly even though I don't remember seeing them. Can wanting something make you know what it is?

# Wednesday, May 25
## 5:50 p.m.

Before Simon and I had our fight, I gave him my cell phone number. Today, he texted me that he was sorry and asked me to come back to school. So I went. He was waiting for me in the yard. He said he wasn't kidding about his dad being in jail, but he didn't want to go into it. Then he said that he knows it's not my fault I say the wrong thing sometimes. I obviously try hard and I'm brave.

I wanted to explain that I hadn't said the wrong thing at all. But I didn't want him to get mad again.

It took me two hours and ten minutes to be able to

look at him without shaking. When I finally did, on the way out of geometry, he smiled.

There was quatre-quarts cake again for lunch, but no Gilberte. I haven't seen her since the first day. I am frustrated by her hiding.

In the cafeteria, I sat with Simon and his friend Marianne, who has very long straight shiny black hair, with purple streaks. Her hair moves like a single piece of cloth. It must be nice to hide behind.

Marianne took a picture of my moth sneakers under the table. She asked if she could post it. I said sure. I didn't ask her specifically where she was going to post it.

There are some things I am very precise about. Posting is not one of them. It's a thing you can obsess on but can't control. Posting happens to you. Like weather.

"Can I tag you?" she asked.

I nodded.

She started to work her phone. "What's your Instagram?" she asked.

"I don't have one."

"Facebook?"

"Sorry."

"Snapchat?"

I shook my head.

"Wait, are you even on anything?" she asked.

"Leave him alone," said Simon.

"What, I just asked a question!" She was still looking at her phone.

"I said, leave him alone!" Simon yelled.

I recognized his anger as inappropriate. Marianne was not being hostile to me. She was asking me a simple question.

"It's okay," I said. "Marianne is not bothering me. She's curious. That's all."

"Fine!" Simon slammed his water glass down on the table and some drops splattered onto my cake. "You're welcome, Martin!"

I watched the moisture soak into the cake. I stared at the damp spots. I did not understand why Simon was first angry at Marianne and now angry at me all over again. I thought maybe I was supposed to thank him for something, which was the reason he was saying "You're welcome" in a sarcastic tone. I wasn't sure though. I wished Maeva was here to help with cues. I tried to think what hints she might give me. I came up empty.

Simon stood up and took a step away from the table.

Marianne turned and grabbed his wrist. Her black hair swished. She had striped nails. She said, "Calm down."

Simon broke away from her and walked off.

"I don't understand," I said. Nothing made sense. I had no more appetite.

"Of course you don't understand. It's fucking absurd. It doesn't make any sense," she said.

Whoa, amazing. She had just echoed what I thought: the way Simon gets angry doesn't make sense. Marianne doesn't get it either. I'm not the only one. When you are not by yourself, being confused is a whole different thing. It's not lonely anymore. Once there's more than one outsider, there aren't really any outsiders.

Marianne put her phone down on the table and we both stared at her picture of my shoes.

A minute after he stormed off, Simon came back. "You okay?" he asked.

"I think so," I said.

He laughed. "As long as you're okay. Just don't, you know, ever let people walk on you."

"I wasn't walking on him," Marianne said.

"Can this be over now?" I asked.

They both laughed. My appetite came back.

## 10:10 p.m.

This evening, I tried to tell Elisabeth and Mom about my day. We were on the terrace. They were drinking wine.

I was eating wrinkled black olives. I didn't tell them about Gilberte and the way she has vanished. I wanted to make them happy by explaining that I had a decent time at school, and that lunch wasn't bad in the end.

"Something was hidden in that golden cake, but I couldn't figure out what," I said. "I sat there in the lunch-room, immobile, watching and breathing, trying to lift my thoughts beyond the image and the odor."

"Use your own fucking words!" Elisabeth yelled. Something was wrong with her. Her gentleness was gone. "Stop quoting all the time!"

Mom told her to go easy. Mom was frowning at me while she talked.

I tried to keep logical. "I wasn't quoting Marcel exactly. When he talked about objects hiding certain meanings, he wasn't talking about pound cake. He was talking about three other things: a rooftop, the reflection of sunlight on a stone, and the scent of trees and flowers along a path. There's a difference."

"Just stop!" Elisabeth snapped. Then she took such a big gulp of her rosé that she choked and teared up. She's not usually like this.

I was acting especially annoying, but I couldn't stop. "Hey, I stayed through lunch again today," I said. "That's progress."

Mom took a big loud breath. Then she picked up an olive and checked it out. She has bony fingers like tree bark. Her fingers were trembling, but only a little. Without tasting it, she put the olive down on her small napkin. "Tell us about the boy who is showing you around," she said.

That gave me an idea. I ran upstairs to my collection of postcards, which are all of the paintings in *Search*. I found the Bellini. I ran downstairs, went outside, and showed it to them. "This is him," I said. "Simon. Mahomet II. Only Bloch is younger. I mean, Simon is younger. Once he grows a goatee, they will be the same person."

"Are you that clueless?" asked Elisabeth. Her neck and cheeks got flushed. "Can you only think about yourself?"

I have no idea what to do with questions like this, which are actually challenges. To escape Elisabeth's anger, I looked out at the sunset. I managed a sympathetic frown. But I couldn't aim the frown at her because I couldn't look in her direction when she was upset like this. So my "appropriate facial expression" was wasted on the open sky.

Elisabeth kept going. "All you can do is be self-referential all the time. Think about someone outside yourself! There's a world out here. Everything isn't about you."

My groaning was coming on. When I groan, my guts go taut and start to vibrate. They make the sound of an out-of-tune violin. I've mostly learned to keep the groaning inside, but sometimes it gets too loud and I have to let it out. Mom hates it when I groan. So I tried very hard not to do it by yelling instead.

What I yelled was true. "Technically," I yelled, "I'm not self-referential. I am referencing a book that is very important to me."

"There's no difference! You are wasting your beautiful life on some random obsession for an old book." Elisabeth's voice got softer and shakier. "Please, Martin. Get real." Then she grabbed her wineglass and went inside. Once she was no longer looking at me, I finally got up the nerve to watch her back disappearing through the red doorway. She was wearing a pair of white shorts with a pattern of blue pineapples that she sewed herself and a soft gray T-shirt. I could tell from her hunching shoulders that she was going to cry.

I couldn't help it: I dropped my head to my chest and groaned. The sound came bursting out of me like steam that has been pent up.

Mom looked away into the setting sun, taking breaths

loud enough for me to hear through my groaning. These are her yoga breaths. They help her to steady herself when I drive her crazy or when one of her actors is being difficult.

After ten breaths, she turned her head to me in a jerky, mechanical way. She forced herself to do it against her body's will (I should know because I force my body into uncomfortable situations all the time). She lifted my chin and then took my shoulders in her hands and found my eyes with hers. I could see her effort to connect.

Then, suddenly, the skin around her eyes crinkled, like leather. She jokes that this expression makes her look tough and scares people on set, but I have a very different reaction. When she crinkles her gaze, she is interested in me, and I want to hold on to her interest. She is watching me the way you watch someone important as they walk toward you. She is curious to see what I will do. This makes me want to do something.

The sleeve of her blouse, which was thin white linen, got picked up by a breeze and brushed against my face. It felt amazing. I stopped groaning.

"Martin," she said gently, "Elisabeth loves you very much. She worries about you because she loves you. It's normal. Can you understand why?"

Then my mind started to work. It went backward to

pick up on something Elisabeth had said. She had said that everything wasn't about me. I now realized that this was a key phrase.

Having a mind that loops can be a useful thing. Sometimes someone else's words will return to show me what I missed the first time around. Marcel calls this "an epiphany." Only for him, it usually happens through smell or taste. For me, epiphanies come mostly in echoes.

"Is it possible that this isn't about me?" I asked Mom. "Elisabeth did say everything isn't about *you*. I mean, she said everything isn't about *me*." I was only repeating Elisabeth's words, but I was onto something big. "Her problem tonight is about her and not about me at all."

Mom let go of my shoulders and moved her head back to get a new angle on me. Then she broke into a smile and started to laugh. "You're right. Talk about self-referential, sweet Martin. You are absolutely right. Elisabeth isn't upset because of you. It's that stupid boy, Jason. He broke up with her this morning."

We stayed on the terrace for twenty-five more minutes. I now believed that Mom forgave me for saying that Simon looks like Bloch from *Search*. She also forgave me for reminding her about the quatre-quarts cakes that used to mess up the kitchen all the time. Whenever she forgives me, I get hopeful that she will forgive Papa too.

Although I was worried about Elisabeth being left by Jason, I was relieved that no one was angry at me after all. I wondered if this meant Elisabeth could date Arthur the art director. I said this to Mom, and she said that Arthur the art director is not a good choice for Elisabeth because he is twice her age.

"So he's thirty-six years, six months, and eight days?" I asked.

"Oh God, Martin! It's not that bad. He's at least twenty-five, though."

"Did Jason call Elisabeth to break up with her or did he text her?"

"I'm not sure," she answered. "Your sister told me he did it over the phone. That's all I know."

"Layla says that telephones can be instruments of torture."

"But we do need them, I'm afraid," Mom said.

"We are both right," I said. "Telephones can be instruments of torture, and we need them."

If there is one thing that *Search* has taught me, it's that there is usually more than one truth.

# Thursday, May 26
## 10:10 a.m.

Elisabeth came into my room with a glass of orange juice to apologize for blowing up at me. I didn't feel like talking to her, though, because I was listening to the flies buzzing through my window. They were performing a little concert for me: "the chamber music of summer."

The sound of flies brings back summer in my memory, like it did for Marcel. Flies are the "certification of summer's return."

I did not want their buzzing interrupted. So I said, "Thank you for the orange juice," very quietly, hoping

Elisabeth would read my cue the way she has taught me to read other people's cues.

Elisabeth didn't understand my message or hear the music of my flies. "Please don't shut yourself up from us," she said, sadly.

I wished I could answer her, but I couldn't pull my concentration away from the fly music, even for my sister.

Eventually, she shrugged her shoulders and went out of the room, closing the door softly behind her. I was grateful. A slam would have ruined everything.

After twenty-two more minutes, the concert ended. Maybe the sun got too strong for the flies.

No matter where the flies go when they stop singing, they will come back again and again, and make their music over and over. This knowledge makes me free.

I am free. This is what Layla and her activists are trying to tell me. This "locked" personality of mine is the creation of all the people who watch me from the outside. Inside, I'm not locked at all.

# Saturday, May 28
## 7:55 p.m.

Today was hot. Simon texted me at 10:00 a.m. that he was going to the town pool. He would be there around noon. He asked if I wanted to come. He said we could eat there. I said yes.

Mom said it was great that Simon reached out. She smiled her open smile. "I'm happy for you, Martin," she said as she hugged me. Even though she has good self-control, Mom's someone who doesn't mask her emotions. She says that in her line of work, you have to be very vocal. After she hugged me, she started to cry. She said it was because she was so happy. Then a car came to get her to take her to the set. She won't be back until very late because the big stars come today. The last thing she said before she drove off was that she will need her yoga breaths today to deal with the stars. This was a joke. Then she winked at me through the car window.

Elisabeth took me in the Smart car to the pool, which is outdoors, surrounded by grass. She was very quiet while she drove. She might have been thinking about Jason breaking up with her.

The pool is twenty-five meters long, with six lane lines. It is divided so that half is for lap swimming and half is for splashing and messing around. Elisabeth came to the poolside with me to make sure I was going to be okay. I saw many towels of too many different colors spread around on the concrete and the grass. Some towels had bodies on them, some were blank. I couldn't see a pattern. The towels scared me. I couldn't look for more than a few seconds. I stared at my feet. My feet are skinny. I was wearing blue Havaianas flip-flops.

I was sure there were people around who would recognize me from school and expect something in return. This idea pressured me. The screaming and splashing were way too loud. I needed silence. I put on my cap and goggles. I started to swim. Elisabeth understood. She waved to me in the water. Then she left to go study in a café she likes in town.

I love to swim laps. What the repetition does is open me up. It flows with no breaks. It's like I am going somewhere fast. It's a thing that Marcel calls "the illusion of fertility."

I did mostly freestyle, with a cooldown of breaststroke. When I got out of the pool, Simon was waiting for me. I looked at his striped white-and-blue trunks and at his chest, which was very thin, and then at his face.

We did our volley of *"Ça va?" "Oui, ça va. Ça va?" "Ça va."* They had no special meaning.

"You've been swimming for over an hour," he said. "You must be really hungry."

"You must be really hungry, yes," I said.

"No, *you* must be really hungry. I'm talking about *you*, not *me*. I've been lying on my towel smoking for the past hour. I'm hungry, but I can't be as hungry as you."

I could have made it clear that, yes, *I* was hungry, but I figured he had already done it for me, and I was thankful.

We went to stand in the line at the snack bar. When I read the menu, I saw that there were crêpes here. Simon hadn't mentioned crêpes in his text. I don't usually like surprises, but this was not an upsetting one. I ordered two crêpes, one with ham and cheese, one with Nutella. Then I offered to buy Simon his lunch. I often buy people

73

lunch. Layla says this gives me an aura of glamour, but I do it because Mom gives me plenty of money, and I usually have more than other people.

Simon said thank you, that he would get me lunch next time. The French for taking someone out is *Je t'invite*, which means "I invite you." Simon said, *"Je t'invite la prochaine fois,"* which means "I'll take you out next time."

No one had ever said this to me before. I looked into his Mahomet II face and said, "Okay."

Layla would say that Simon was being nice to me because he is a moth who has found out that the stars are arriving in town today. I don't care. I like him.

Suddenly, I knew Gilberte was here. It was her eyes on my back again. I turned around to see her pulling herself up from the water onto the side of the pool. She was wearing a white swim cap. Her blue goggles were up on her head. She had red rings pressed in the skin around her eyes, which were now black. To have such deep rings, she must have been swimming for a while. This meant that we had been in the water at the same time.

Her bathing suit was a white two-piece. Her breasts were smaller than I had been thinking, but I didn't mind. Her skin was brown. As her body rose up into the sunlight, beads of water made rainbows all over her.

I smiled, and she smiled back. Then she walked away into the towels.

I asked Simon, who was picking up our crêpes from the counter, if he had seen Gilberte. I knew Gilberte was not her name, but I could not let go of it.

"Who?" he asked. "I hope for her sake that's not her name. It's the twenty-first century, Martin."

I couldn't talk about her anymore.

After lunch, Simon had to go. He has a little brother he has to take care of so his mom can go to work. She's a checker in a supermarket. I said thank you for getting me to come to the pool. He said I was a good swimmer. I no longer feel any anger from him.

I texted Elisabeth to come get me.

With Simon gone and the bright towels moving in closer, I was nervous. So I took *Search* from my bag to read the passage where Marcel realizes that people are "opaque" because we try to see them with our "senses" and not our "sensibility." Only people we look at with "sensibility" can become "intimates." I smiled inside because Gilberte, no matter what her actual name is, is already an intimate for me. Safe inside my bubble because she has always been here.

While I was watching through the fence for the Smart

car to pull into the parking lot, I tried to find the courage to step into the towels to look for Gilberte. Every time I glanced at the crowd, it started to writhe. I wanted badly to escape it, but I also wanted badly to dive in and find her.

Papa has explained this tension. He calls it "conflict," and he says it is the motor of literature. In that moment, I just wanted the conflict to go away. And it did. Because Gilberte tapped me on the shoulder.

"*Salut. Ça va?*" she asked. Her voice is both hoarse and musical. Her *Ça va?* did not sound generic. It sounded like she might be playing Papa's and my *Ça va* game. Like she was really saying, "Are you happy now that we've met?"

"*Oui, Gilberte, ça va.*" My *Ça va* meant "Yes, I'm very happy."

She laughed, asking how I came up with that funny name, Gilberte. Even if I don't care about getting teased, I still recognize teasing, and she was definitely teasing me, but not viciously. She looked over into the crowd of kids, probably at her friends, who were watching us. I had to finally admit that she is visible to everyone and is not my personal ghost.

I told her my name was Martin. Holding out her hand, she said, "I guess I'm Gilberte. Nice to meet you, Martin."

The moment she said my name, I became somebody. So this was *our* game.

"Are you coming to school on Monday?" she asked. Her freckles were dazzling but not strange. This was definitely not a first impression. I might not know her body so well, but I know her face. Otherwise I wouldn't be able to look straight at her like this.

"Of course," I said. "I'll see you Monday." As though there was never any doubt. Like I was always up for a school full of strangers.

The girl who has been nothing but a name with a picture attached is now a person I will find again on Monday.

I swelled up with confidence. I pictured going into the *boulangerie* and asking the woman behind the counter for two madeleines, smiling right at her instead of staring into the pastry case at the chocolate swirls decorating the tops of the mille-feuilles, which are called "Napoleons" in English.

Layla says that fantasy is the first step to action.

Elisabeth pulled into the parking lot. "That's my sister picking me up. See you Monday," I said to Gilberte.

"See you Monday."

# Sunday, May 29
## 1:00 p.m.

Elisabeth has a poster of an aerial photograph of the Chenonceau castle in her room at home. I've been looking at it for years. It has six arches over the river, and it makes a perfect reflection in the water. It has three stories, four chimneys, and two turrets. Elisabeth used to say she wanted to live there so that she could sleep in a canopy bed in a room full of Flemish tapestries with unicorns on them. Now that she's older, she doesn't mention these things anymore.

This morning, she drove me to the château to watch

a scene being shot in the king's bedroom. I asked her if she remembers wanting to be a princess.

"Sort of," she said. She didn't sound annoyed, but she sighed.

I had this idea that I would try to make Elisabeth feel better about things with Jason, because she is the one who tries to make me feel better most of the time. They call this "reciprocity."

I can tell Elisabeth is unhappy because she's frowning a lot, and not the kind of frown where she is concentrating on memorizing chemistry, but the kind of frown where the corners of her eyes get wet.

I said: "Try not to worry about the breakup with Jason because Jason is a twit."

She laughed for a second, then the laugh stopped and she started in on a teaching moment. "Martin, can you come up with another word for Jason? *Twit* is Mom's word for him. Mom said at breakfast that he was acting like a twit. What is *your* word?"

To find my word for Jason, I started going through *Search* in my mind.

Since I can't really look at Jason, I didn't have much to go on. But Elisabeth has told me that there is another girl involved. She is an actress and perhaps more glamorous than Elisabeth, who is beautiful but sews her own clothes and wants to be a doctor for kids with mental problems. It hit me. Jason is a snob.

There are tons of snobs in *Search*.

My first idea was to tell Elisabeth that Jason was a snob too. Then I remembered I should be trying to make my own cakes instead of only lining up my ingredients. So I squeezed together the ingredients in my brain. This is what I came up with: "Jason is nothing but a twit-snob."

"What?"

"Well, Mom is right that he is acting like a twit. But I need to be original, so I shouldn't copy her. And Jason makes me think of one of the snobs in *Search* called Legrandin. Legrandin thinks he's better than Marcel and his family. He prefers duchesses the way Jason prefers actresses. And he's very stupid. So Jason is both a twit and a snob, and I've made my own version of the two things. Twit-snob."

I had a moment of panic that Elisabeth would decide her teaching moment had failed because I wasn't saying anything that hadn't been said before. But she didn't get her angry flush or her disappointed frown. She reached over to the passenger seat, squeezed my knee, and said something she had not said before. "Never change."

This was confusing. They are always trying to change me.

### 11:40 p.m.

I was going to make cassoulet today from a new cookbook that Mom bought in town. Cassoulet is a French stew of white beans with sausages and duck legs. The cookbook is a French classic called *Je sais cuisiner* by Ginette Mathiot. It is bright yellow with a photograph of Ginette Mathiot in an apron, surrounded by traditional dishes—a roast, a ratatouille, and a clafoutis—along with some raw vegetables for decoration. Mom bought the book so that I would branch out from the cassoulet recipe I always use, which is from Julia Child, who looks bigger and stronger than Ginette Mathiot. Julia Child also doesn't put her picture on the cover of her books. Her books have a simple, soothing pattern on the outside, with Julia's picture tucked inside, on the jacket flap.

A group of twenty-one cast and crew members were here for dinner tonight. I said I would cook for them because Mom had a full day of shooting. While I was prepping, I imagined Gilberte tasting my food. I had soaked my white beans overnight to get them soft and ready. And I had baked two quatre-quarts cakes for dessert in order to have something comfortable in the meal, in case the new cassoulet was a disaster. I was nervous about an unfamiliar recipe, but I'd given myself this goal.

At dinner, a man's voice described the type of places Mom picks when she's on location. He was making a toast. The man's voice said, "Samantha, you usually get the most homey and least expensive place by a factor of five, and it ends up the place everyone is drawn to, where all the faithful gather." It was the same voice that had offered me more asparagus the other night. I decided to call the speaker "Asparagus Man."

People raised their glasses and drank. Asparagus Man said, "Here's to the reigning queen of Chenonceau. Diane de Poitiers and Catherine de Médicis don't have anything on our Samantha de Mitchell."

Mom's last name is Mitchell. Elisabeth changed her name to Mitchell too. I've kept Papa's last name, which is Dubois. I'm Martin Dubois.

I wanted to add to the toast. I wanted to say that Mom is exactly like Marcel's grandmother because she favors old things that somehow educate you about the past, and she's "allergic to vulgarity." This is why we are renting a cottage with no air-conditioning instead of a big renovated house with marble bathrooms. Mom hates marble bathrooms, unless they are the old-fashioned black-and-white kind with art deco faucets. They don't have those here. I wished I could stand up and say these things out loud but I couldn't.

Asparagus Man stopped toasting Mom and sat down.

Mom's cast and crew were crowded around folding tables on our little terrace eating cassoulet, made by me, and salad, made by Elisabeth and our housekeeper, Bernadette, when they could be at a restaurant with Michelin stars or at a catered party at one of the actors' big houses. Baxter Wolff, for example, is staying in a renovated manor house with many bathrooms (most likely marble) and a big staff. But he has spent his evening having dinner here, on our terrace with mismatched chairs and all different-sized plates and bowls. He has even had seconds of my cassoulet.

I ended up caving and making my usual recipe, but I didn't mention this to Mom. She can't tell because, even though I followed Julia Child as faithfully as ever, the cassoulet tastes different from at home. The duck meat here is gamier. And the rosemary is much stronger.

I did tell Bernadette that I was following my tradition, and she said she approved because it is rarely a good idea to innovate. Bernadette looks about seventy-five to me, but Mom says she is younger and that she is weathered. She has thick, round shoulders and fingers that are as knobby as old trees.

By the end of the evening, there were eight people left at the party. They are what *Search* calls the *intimes*. Every one of Mom's movies has its *petit clan*, its tight little group of people who spend most of their time together. Elisabeth calls this a "hothouse environment." She says it leads to a lot of affairs.

What I know about affairs, I have learned from the second section of *Search*, which is all about Mr. Swann's obsession with Odette de Crécy. It takes place in the novel's past, before Gilberte is born, back when her parents are having an affair in Paris.

The first time Mr. Swann sees Odette, he doesn't even find her pretty. The second time he sees her, she reminds him of a woman called Zephora, from the Bible, in a fresco by Botticelli that he's seen in the Sistine Chapel. That's when he falls in love. I have a picture of Zephora in my postcard collection.

When Mr. Swann says he "knows" a person or a place, it is because he has found a way to connect them to art. He doesn't see people as their original selves. He sees them as Old Master faces. That's why, even though she is not very smart or nice and she has a gray complexion,

Odette casts a spell on Mr. Swann. As soon as he notices that she looks like the woman in the fresco, he gets obsessed with her. It's all about references. Maybe Mr. Swann is autistic.

Asparagus Man is different from Mr. Swann. Mr. Swann is aware that he is not well adjusted, and this makes him suffer. Asparagus Man thinks he is well adjusted. He does not seem to be suffering at all. But he is not well adjusted.

When Asparagus Man made his toast to Mom tonight, he was proud. He had a picture of Mom in his head that was very selfish, even if he was pretending it was for everyone else.

I wished I could look at Asparagus Man directly. A few glances showed me that his goatee has grown longer since our restaurant dinner, an asparagus tip goatee. And because his black T-shirt was so tight, I could see that his shoulders are very thick.

Asparagus Man is not a complete stranger. He is a familiar sound, color, even a smell. But not yet a person. And here he is claiming to know Mom better than the rest of us, to tell us who she is. This is not okay.

At dessert, when he got up again and raised another glass and said, "Sam, you sure make us feel loved," Mom smiled her warm smile at him. This made me nauseated.

Marcel says that "a fantasy of love is often a fantasy of place." Asparagus Man was happy on our terrace on a beautiful summer night in the French countryside. This place was making him think he might love Mom. But Mom is not his to love.

When Asparagus Man asked me what was in my cassoulet, I answered "Beans." When I didn't make eye contact, he must have assumed I was rude. Although Mom has probably explained to him about me. In any case, he didn't try to talk to me anymore.

I decided to try to stop focusing on Mom and Asparagus Man and to watch Elisabeth and Arthur the art director instead. I saw that Elisabeth was laughing in the way that shows her gums, which means she is not trying to hide them. She was wearing a black sleeveless dress that she made, with silver buttons down the front. Three of the buttons were undone instead of the usual two.

Arthur's furry outline was becoming friendlier. While he talked to Elisabeth, he took smiling bites of his cake. She was also eating her cake in between talking and laughing. This symmetry between them gave me a good feeling.

When I looked over at Mom again, the good feeling was ruined. This is what she was doing: she was pretending to laugh, silently, with her face in her hands, at something Asparagus Man had said. She was showing him with a sign that he was funny. She was not being truthful. I recognize this from a description of the fake laugh of a horrible phony named Madame Verdurin.

*Search* was under my knee on my chair. I took it out and turned to the page with the laugh. Since I have certain pages folded over, it was easy to find.

> She released a little cry, closed her bird-like eyes and plunged her face into her hands, not leaving anything in sight, she seemed to be forcing herself to repress and stifle a laugh which, were she to abandon herself to it, would have driven her into a faint.

I've learned that it is rude to take out *Search* at the table. But everyone was busy talking. They were yelling about the hundreds of fireflies that were starting to flicker around us. I figured they wouldn't notice me reading. They didn't.

When Mom and Elisabeth served third helpings of dessert to the little clan, Fuchsia started laughing about how she was going to have to either stop eating this cake or throw it up.

Even though I should recognize Fuchsia's comment as a joke, the idea of Papa's and my quatre-quarts as throw up made me unhappy. I had to leave the table. But I didn't want to be inappropriate to Mom's little clan by bolting away. So I decided to announce that I was tired.

Only, because I was nervous, it came out wrong.

"Excuse me. You're tired. You need to sleep," I said too loudly.

Mom winced.

Before anyone could realize I'd made a mistake, Elisabeth saved me from across the table. "You're right, I am tired and I do need to sleep," she said. "No one can read me like my brother. Let's get up to bed, Martin. We both have to study tomorrow."

Arthur smiled at her through his beard.

I looked up at Mom and saw her smiling too.

I wanted to be straight with Mom. "Actually," I blurted, "I meant to say that I was tired."

"Well, who says there's a law against meaning two things at once?" asked Elisabeth. "It's called a double entendre, right?"

"Right," echoed Arthur.

I nodded. "Yes, it is."

Asparagus Man winked at Mom. She may have winked back. I hope not.

88

As I was leaving, Asparagus Man, pointing to my book, asked if I was going upstairs to wait for my mother's kiss. Asparagus Man was trying to show us that he was familiar with Proust, since Marcel does wait in agony for his mother's goodnight kiss for a lot of the first section. What he showed was that he doesn't know anything about me, since it's Papa I am waiting for.

I did not respond to Asparagus Man.

I suddenly wished Papa and I hadn't been so inconsiderate with our messes when we baked together. I pictured our kitchen at home, dusted in flour, the mixer paddle dripping batter into the sink full of dishes.

There is a buttery, sweet smell from the oven. Mom looks around at the chaos and sighs.

I'm very careful these days to clean up after myself in the kitchen, but I'm afraid it's too late.

# Tuesday, May 31
## 7:00 a.m.

Yesterday, I was supposed to see Gilberte at school. I had this idea that we were going to wander off to Chenonceau together, straight into the poster from Elisabeth's wall. I couldn't focus on anything else.

When I didn't see her in history class or in the hallway or the cafeteria or the yard, I asked Simon if he had an idea where the girl I call Gilberte was. We were outside after lunch. He laughed at me about the old-fashioned name. He said I must be imagining her. There is no Gilberte in this school.

I should have told him she was the girl from the pool in the white bikini, but I couldn't. My chest was squeezing into itself. I didn't mind Simon teasing me, but I did mind getting no answer. My breathing got shallow. I got scared I might groan.

Then Simon changed the subject. He asked if I could mention him to Mom because he is going to go for the casting call tomorrow morning for extras in her crowd scenes. He said he knew me well enough to ask, which was confusing. I stopped trying to look at his face and went back to looking at his shoes, like on the first day of school. His shoes are always the same black Doc Martens, except for when he wears his brandless flip-flops at the pool.

I wanted to believe him that we were becoming friends, so that it was okay to ask for favors. Like it was a sign of trust. But he was ignoring the thing *I* was trying to ask *him*. We were both totally focused on our own favors.

I told him I didn't know about any casting call for extras. He kept saying that he was going to go try out and that it always helps to have a connection. Then he asked me if I'd seen Gloria Seegar yet. I was so nervous that I repeated his question. Twice. "Have you seen her yet?

Have you seen her yet?" Then finally I managed to tell him yes, I had seen Gloria Seegar. All I wanted was to learn about Gilberte.

"Why are you teasing me? Pretending not to know about the casting?" he yelled. "You're acting like a snob." He walked away from me.

At lunchtime, I didn't eat. I didn't even go to the cafeteria. I stood in the concrete schoolyard, waiting for her even though it was pointless. I waited like Mr. Swann used to wait for Odette on nights when it was too late to hope. I stood there watching the pigeons "posed like antique sculptures waiting patiently to frame her image." She did not come.

When the bell rang for class to start, I didn't go back inside the school building. I texted Layla that I hated France. It was 4:00 a.m. Layla's time so she shouldn't have gotten back to me for a while. But she immediately shot me a video of her hands on the keyboard playing "You Can't Always Get What You Want" by the Rolling Stones.

Layla is a gifted pianist. She has a perfect ear. She can play anything she hears right back, like theme music, movie scores, and commercial jingles. But the songs she is into are all really old ones by the Beatles and the Rolling Stones. She says that these songs "run the gamut of

human communication and can convey any message."
Layla really talks like that. She has a setup for her phone
on her piano so that she can show you her fingers while
she plays. Although she can play anything, the classical
music I listen to doesn't mean much to her.

**Thanks**, I texted back.

**You're welcome. Do you think our phones are in-
struments of communication or torture?**

Today, I am going to school again, even though yesterday Gilberte never showed. She broke the agreement
we made at the pool. Maybe she will come today. Or
maybe not. She might not take our agreement as seri-
ously as I do. Marcel had this same problem with his
Gilberte too.

4:46 p.m.

Before school, I had breakfast with Elisabeth. It was
sunny. I found her at the table on the terrace, staring
into space instead of doing her chemistry on her laptop, which was open beside her giant molecule book. I
brought the bread, which was *pain de campagne*, the cut-
ting board, the knife, the plates and spoons and butter
knives, the napkins, the butter, and the rhubarb jam. I
made her coffee in the metal percolator. I warmed milk

for her coffee. I got myself a glass of orange juice because I am not supposed to drink coffee.

"Wow, thanks, Martin," she said.

She was wearing her black cotton bathrobe that is very worn and thin. Her hair was down, which is happening more and more these days. It made soft curls where it hit her shoulders. I wondered if she forgot to put it up because she was thinking about Arthur.

Wondering about people's motivations is called "conjecture."

I decided to ask her about Arthur. "Elisabeth," I said, "you don't look sad about Jason anymore. Is this because you are starting to be with Arthur?"

"Arthur is so much cooler than Jason."

"How do you know that right away? How can you be sure you're not making it up?"

"Because it's obvious that Arthur is a secure person. Jason is an opportunist. He's always trying to figure out how he can get ahead, but his idea of what's 'ahead' is always changing. He cares too much about appearances. That's why he's dating a skinny actress now."

I did not argue that something that seems obvious doesn't have to be true. So I said I agreed about Jason being unreliable and vain. Then I asked her to please explain how Arthur is a secure person.

"Well," Elisabeth said. "Take the way he deals with Mom on the movie. He totally respects her vision of what it should look like, but he also has his own vision. He's not threatened by her, so he doesn't try to act smarter than her like some younger guys would. He doesn't lose sight of his own opinions either. He's like a scientist. He weighs all the possibilities and keeps them in his head at the same time until he figures out which one is right."

"You're a scientist too," I said, loving the parallel.

"That's part of why we get along so well."

"Were you sure about him the very moment you saw him?"

"I was, but I couldn't see it because I assumed he was way too old for me. Seven years seems like a lot. Then, one day we were talking and it was like all of a sudden it was clear." She looked at me. She sipped her coffee. "Why are you asking me? Not that I mind or anything. Can you tell if you like him yet?"

She'd asked two totally different questions. I answered them one at a time, out of order. "First of all, I am starting to like him. I'm going to make a real effort to look through all the facial hair next time I see him. Second of all, I am asking because I am looking for new ways to make friends."

She smiled and started eating.

The flies were making their music around the rhubarb jam, which, thankfully, Asparagus Man has not been around to steal. It's almost gone, though. I'll get some more for Mom. They sell it at the bakery where the madeleines are. Where I'm going to take Gilberte.

I keep having visions of her eating.

After breakfast, Elisabeth changed from her bathrobe into her hawthorn dress and drove me to school.

The sky was cloudless. Gilberte had to finally come.

She didn't. And the sky got cloudy as the day went on.

## 11:30 p.m.

Not long after Papa went away to prison, Mom took a trip to Paris to scout some locations for a movie she never ended up shooting. To cheer me up, she brought me home a re-creation of Proust's magic lantern that she found in a museum, the Musée d'Orsay. It was supposed to project the same colorful medieval prince and princess on my walls that Marcel saw in his room. She said it would change the color of my light the way it changed his. When she pulled it out of her carry-on bag, she was super excited. Elisabeth explained afterward that Mom was trying to show me that she understood my *Search* obsession too. She wanted to prove that losing Papa wasn't such a disaster after all.

The magic lantern terrified me. I hated the colors changing all the time in unpredictable ways. I hated the idea that my own room could suddenly become a different place. I threw the lantern away in the kitchen garbage.

Mom cried.

I told her not to worry. Marcel was scared of his lantern too.

# Wednesday, June 1
## 6:15 p.m.

I asked Elisabeth to drop me off early at school this morning.

"Are you meeting your Gilberte girl?" Elisabeth asked while we drove.

"I hope so," I said. "She hasn't been there for two days, but maybe she will show up today."

"Does Simon know what's going on with her?"

"Simon doesn't know any Gilberte."

"What do you mean he doesn't know her?"

"He says there is nobody called Gilberte at the *lycée*. But I've met her, and so has he. I've seen him talking to her. So that's not true."

"Don't you think this girl probably has another name?"

These questions made me tight inside.

Elisabeth changed the subject. "How is Simon?" she asked.

I was grateful to stop talking about Gilberte's name.

"Simon is going to be an extra in Mom's crowd scenes. I asked her to pick him, and she did. She doesn't agree that he looks like the Bellini portrait, though. She almost didn't recognize him from what I said. But I'd given her the right name, so it all worked out."

"That's nice of you to help out a friend."

"I'm trying."

We stopped talking and drove.

After Elisabeth dropped me off, I stood in the school-yard in a spot where I could see both entrances. I couldn't leave or stop looking around because Gilberte might come from any direction. Marcel would call this yard "an immense expanse of space and time."

Kids started to trickle in like extras. A lot of them were smoking in the street, stepping on the butts just before they came into the schoolyard. Nobody I know at The Center smokes, but I have gotten used to the cigarettes here more quickly than I thought I could. I can look at the smokers as long as I don't have to look directly into their faces. I wonder if, when I am old like Marcel at the end of *Search*, the clothes they are wearing now, the Converse, the Doc Martens, the skinny jeans, and the Hilfiger T-shirts, will have become beautiful, lost things from the past.

I was thinking about changing fashions when I saw Gilberte approaching. She was not smoking. She was wearing a black cotton sundress with a thin rope belt and gladiator sandals. Her hair was pulled back in a ponytail. I realized that her hair wasn't as red as I've been picturing it. More blond.

I went right up to her, keeping my eyes up, even though her feet are pretty.

"*Ça va?*" she asked, meaning, "Have you missed me?"

"*Ça va,*" I answered, meaning, "I've been looking for you for two days."

"Where have you been?" I asked. This is proof that I know Gilberte well. I could never ask a stranger such a direct question.

"My baby sister was sick and my parents had to go to work, so I had to stay home with her because she couldn't go to her day care with a fever. Normally my mom or dad would have skipped work, but they've been doing some important planting."

"My friend Simon has a baby brother he takes care of,"
I said. This wasn't a normal way to have a conversation,
but I needed to make the link.

"I know," she said.

"You know Simon?"

"Yes. Of course. That's how I met you."

"Well, he told me he has no idea who you are."

I recognized confusion in her eyes, which I saw, for
sure, were not blue. They weren't black either. My Gilberte's eyes were brown. Marcel's Gilberte does not, ever
in the book, have brown eyes. I am going to overlook this.

"He's such a joker," she finally said. She sounded annoyed. I hoped she was not annoyed at me, but I'm not
always a great judge of other people's irritation. I can be
more annoying than I feel. So I worried I might have offended her by revealing Simon's lie or joke or whatever
it was. Only it was Simon's fault for pretending not to
know Gilberte.

Now I realized that when Gilberte first talked to me
at the pool, it was because I was hanging out with Simon.
She was friends with Simon. She paid attention to me
because I was with him. And she wondered who I could
be. The new boy? The American? The famous movie director's son? The special-ed kid?

Certain things were beginning to fall into place. But they were knocking other things out of order. Although it was confusing, our situation was cool because it was like a novel. The idea came to me that Simon must love Gilberte too, that this was why he was throwing me off track with lies. Of course, Simon and I weren't alone. Everyone in town must be in love with her. I pictured boys and men all around, checking her out through car windows. I must be jealous. Like Mr. Swann. It's a weird feeling. There's some pain. It's also exciting because I'm part of something, like a small cloud in a dark storm.

Although I'm not used to sophisticated emotions in myself, I am ready for them from all my reading. It might not look like it, but people like Layla and me are pretty well equipped to deal with melodrama.

"Do you want to sit together at lunch?" Gilberte asked.

"Sure," I said.

"Okay. See you later in the cafeteria."

"Okay."

After math and history, Gilberte found me at the entrance to the cafeteria. She said she was sorry, but she had to grab a sandwich and take off. She needed to go study for a *contrôle*, which is a test. She'd only found out about it this morning on account of missing school these past days. She asked if I was on Facebook. I said no. So she told me her number and I added her to my contacts. I immediately texted her: **coucou from Marcel**. Then I sent another, corrected message: **coucou from Martin**.

**So who are you?** she wrote back. **Marcel or Martin?**

**I'm Martin. Nice to meet you, Gilberte.**

**You think I look like a Gilberte?** she typed. She was smiling, and her freckles—she really does have freckles—glittered.

**Oui.**

**Okay A+**

It took me a while to figure out *A+*. *A+*, or *À plus,* is short for *À plus tard*, which means "Until later" or "See you later." French kids use it the way American kids use *later*, as in "Later, dude."

I'm not so up on abbreviations. Simon seems to have figured this out from the start. He always spells stuff out for me in his texts. To Gilberte I must seem normal enough to be okay with French texting shorthand. I'm flattered.

She said she would text me later about a plan for to-morrow after school. A group of kids might be going to the pool.

After school, to distract myself from the crazy anticipation of Gilberte's text, I put on my headphones, took a walk down the road, and picked a bunch of hawthorns from the bushes. I found some pink blossoms mixed in with the white ones. I put them in a vase on the kitchen table. Their odor is bitter and sweet like almonds. They remind me of something. Everything reminds me of something right now. The whole world is full of meanings.

Back at home, I waited for her message. I was in the kitchen staring at my blank phone screen, smelling the pink and white hawthorns. I was alone. Elisabeth was at the château with Mom, watching a scene that was shooting in one of the bedrooms with the canopies and Flemish tapestries she used to dream about.

I tried to stop myself from imagining what Gilberte might write, because anything that I came up with could never become real. And even if she did send one of the texts I was trying not to write in my head, I would then be upset because it wasn't original.

The phone vibrated. It was Gilberte.

**Piscine demain 17.** Pool tomorrow at 5:00 p.m.

I need to answer her in a way that is poetic, yet cool. I want to make her understand that I have seen her before many times in my dreams, that we are actually meeting again, and not for the first time.

How about, **Like the odor of hawthorn, I keep losing and finding you again**?

Nope. Too flowery. Maybe something about the flow of water in the pool? **The perpetual alliteration between the water, without consistency, which our cupped hands cannot capture, and the clear plastic of our goggles . . .**

Nope. Nope. Nope. That's way too many words. I don't have a model for this. The greatest work in French literature at my fingertips and there's nothing I can use. This is crazy.

Maybe an emoji? A thumbs-up or a smiling face?

No. I can usually rely on emojis, but they don't feel right here.

I need Elisabeth to help me. Or Layla. I message them together: **What should I text the girl of my dreams?**

**Are you talking about Gilberte?** writes Layla, who is familiar with my characters, even though she hasn't read *Search*.

**Yes**, I answer. **Gilberte Swann.**

**How is she?**

**She's great. I need to answer a text from her about meeting at the pool. There's a big public pool here that**

105

is kind of a hangout place. She asked me to go tomorrow. Help!

Now Elisabeth chimes in: **Keep it simple.**

Nothing more from Layla, which is not like her.

Elisabeth's advice to keep it simple appears as a giant poster in my mind. I stare straight at it, search my soul for simplicity, and find it.

I answer Gilberte's text: **A+**

# Thursday, June 2
## 1:15 p.m.

I barely got any sleep last night.

Layla sent me four piano videos. Her fingers danced easily over the black and white keys. The first song was "Michelle" by the Beatles. She wrote a tagline for it: **Sorry, this was the closest I could come to an appropriate love song. Gilberte seems to be an unsung name. How do you explain this?**

The next three songs came with no messages and were in this order: "Wild Horses," "Memory Motel," and "Angie." They came at ninety-minute intervals. Each time, I responded with my usual **thank you**.

Halfway between "Wild Horses" and "Memory Motel,"

I sat up in a panic because I realized that I'd completely missed something major Gilberte had told me. I'd been so into my connection between her baby sister and Simon's baby brother that I hadn't paid attention when she'd said that her parents were "doing some important planting." In between Layla's songs, I suddenly remembered. Questions about planting kept me awake. Are they farmers? Landscape architects? I need to know.

In the third section of *Search*, which happens in Paris, Marcel finally meets Gilberte. They cross paths in the Champs-Élysées, where they both go with their governesses on sunny afternoons. They start hanging out in the same group of kids. He's always taken her for more of a fantasy than a reality. And suddenly she's in his world. He gets curious about every part of her life. His happiness each day depends on whether or not she shows up in the park. He's in love. She's nice to him, but she also makes it clear that she has a lot going on outside the park that he is not part of. She has a whole other life, and this drives him crazy.

Marcel gets fascinated by every detail about Gilberte. He stares at the map of Paris to find the address of her house. He imagines the lives of her parents. Her father, Mr. Swann, starts to seem like a major historical figure.

And Marcel follows her mother, Odette, around on her strolls through the Bois de Boulogne in her fancy clothes.

Marcel starts acting like Mr. Swann did back when he was in love with Odette. He obsesses over the parts of Gilberte's life that he is shut out from. He loses interest in anything that isn't about her. Everything he does is a ploy to get people to talk about her and her parents. He wants to hear their names and cross their paths.

I'm obsessed too. I want to know all about her family. I love the fact that her parents do "planting," even if I'm not sure what kind or what it means. It's exciting to get closer. Because it makes me feel like I could actually touch her. Pull her into me.

My body craves the unknown. I've never craved the unknown before. I've always hidden from it. This is totally new.

And yet there is also something disappointing about the "planting," because planting parents obviously aren't Mr. and Mrs. Swann. The Swanns were not any kind of professional planters. They weren't professional anything. They didn't have jobs. Odette was a "kept woman" before she became Mrs. Swann, and Mr. Swann was just plain rich.

Gilberte does not look rich. She wears cheap clothes,

even if they are fantastic on her. Don't get me wrong, I don't need a rich girl. It's just that not being rich takes Gilberte a step away from *Search*.

Is getting to know Gilberte going to break too much with my story? Worrying about this, I couldn't sleep. I tossed around in my bed. I kept going over stuff.

At 4:00 a.m., I found a new way to think about it: So my Gilberte doesn't match the original. But she can still give me the same emotions that Marcel's Gilberte gave him. This is all I need. The bigger story says that I love everything about her, that I care about all parts of her life and the people she's closest to. Even if they are planters.

By the time Layla played "Angie," I felt a little better about Gilberte. But I still couldn't sleep because there was something else.

Asparagus Man was in our cottage. From not looking at him, I know his voice better than his face. I heard him talking and laughing with Mom after her car and his noisy equipment van pulled up last night at 11:45. Then I never heard him say good-bye from outside my window. I never heard the van start again and then fade away. So, unless I fell deep asleep without realizing it, he is still here. I can't see the driveway from my window to check right now, but I'm positive the stupid black van hasn't left.

This sort of thing has happened a few times before. It doesn't last. Even so, I hate it.

When Elisabeth knocked on my door to wake me up for school this morning, I asked her to come into my room. I told her I couldn't go to school today because I hadn't slept and I needed to rest up for the pool later, at five. Then I asked her if there was a man here.

First Elisabeth came back at me with her own questions: "Why don't you ask Mom yourself?" "Why don't you go down and see?" Then she realized she was being mean because she was in a bad mood. I could tell because she suddenly made her tone more gentle. "Yes, Joe's downstairs having breakfast with Mom. He's actually not that bad. Even so, my guess is you're not up to seeing him right now. Don't freak out. He and Mom will leave soon. They are doing a big garden scene today. He's the head cameraman, in case you were wondering."

All I could think of to say was, "Hide the rhubarb jam! It's almost gone!"

She burst out laughing. At least I was cheering her up.

"We can get more jam, Martin," she reassured me. "They have it in the village. At the bakery. Where they have beautiful madeleines, by the way."

"You have seen the madeleines in the window." I took a beat to try to fix my pronoun from *you* to *I*, but it was no use. "That jam is yours and your mother's. Asparagus Man can have the other kinds. He can have the apricot or the plum. Not the rhubarb."

"Whoa, personal-pronoun alert! Where did *I* go? And what do you mean about asparagus? Who's eating asparagus?"

This was too much.

"Sorry!" I screamed. "I mean the jam is *my—you* know what I mean! It's also Papa's. Papa's rhubarb jam for toast with butter with *me*. You happy with the pronouns now?"

She tried to distract me. "Is that supposed to be Gilberte?" she asked, looking at the postcard I was holding. I was staring at it to block out visions of Asparagus Man in my house.

My postcard is from the Botticelli fresco in the Sistine Chapel called *Events in the Life of Moses*. It shows Zephora, the same Zephora that Mr. Swann pictured when he fell for Odette. She's by a well with her sister. Moses is there too, helping them give water to their sheep. Zephora has big eyes; a delicate face; very pale skin; long, shiny curls; and long, tired cheeks.

"It's a painting of Gilberte's mother, Odette," I said, relieved to be back in the world of facts. "This is what makes Mr. Swann, who is Gilberte's dad, understand that he loves Odette. At first Mr. Swann isn't even attracted to Odette. Then he notices that Odette looks like Zephora from this fresco by Botticelli. He changes his mind and starts to love her. It's magic. At first, Mr. Swann loves Odette because she looks like this painting, but eventually Mr. Swann loves the painting because it is a painting of her. Isn't that cool? Proust calls it transubstantiation!"

"Wow, dude. I'm not sure I follow you. Why do you care so much about Gilberte's mother? Have you even met her mother?"

"I'm very, very interested in her mother."

"Kinky," Elisabeth said.

Then I identified embarrassment followed by a flight instinct. "You sure you're not going to school?" She talked quickly, not even waiting for an answer. "I'll be downstairs working if you change your mind."

There is so much stuff that people don't want to say.

Proust doesn't tell everything in *Search*. He focuses on a few scenes. He goes into such detail that it feels like they have covered years instead of moments. Most everything else that happens is left out, but you don't miss it, the way you don't miss all the stuff that isn't in your favorite painting or all the rooms that aren't in your favorite house. Sometimes the absent stuff turns out to matter in the end. Sometimes it doesn't.

# Friday, June 3
## 6:30 p.m.

Yesterday, even though I didn't go to school, I went to the pool to meet Gilberte. Simon was there too with some other kids.

I felt comfortable enough with Gilberte and Simon that I was able to take in their friends: Georges, Michel, Kevin (that's a popular American name here, from TV), and black-and-purple-haired Marianne. There was the usual volley of *Ça va*, which gave me time to adjust.

The boys are as narrow and hollow-chested as figures from a Giotto painting. It must be all the smoking. Marianne is a bit fuller, but not much. I had already hung out with these kids in the cafeteria, the hallways, and the classrooms at school, so I wasn't freaking. There wasn't nearly as big a crowd at the pool as on the weekend. The towel mosaic around the deck wasn't so hard to get through.

There were a couple of cracks about how I had ditched school but had somehow made it to the pool. I was able to smile at these cracks, which gave me hope. Still, I got nervous. So I put on my goggles and swam some hundreds in individual medley order—butterfly, back, breast, free—while my "friends" splashed around and sunbathed. The pool is twenty-five meters here instead of the American twenty-five yards. This makes it two strokes longer than at home.

One thing that helps me pass in a general-ed world is that I'm coordinated. I'm strong and pretty good at sports. This is thanks to Papa.

When I was diagnosed, the psychologists told my parents that passing a ball back and forth with me was the most basic form of therapy. It forced me to look at the person I was catching from, follow the ball, and again look at the person I was throwing to. Keeping eye contact was key, they said. They also explained that playing catch is something done by two or more people: it's started by one person, finished by another person, and so on. The game would teach me that I was a body separate from my parents and that we could perform tasks by working together.

To Mom and Papa, this ball thing sounded absurdly obvious. Then they tried it. And they saw right away that it wasn't obvious to me at all. That's when they realized that I had no idea what was going on in the world outside me, even though I could sing "Au clair de la lune" perfectly and recite the whole book *Goodnight Moon*.

Papa said that, at first, even throwing me the ball was much too complicated. One of them had to roll it while the other one held me in place to catch it. If I wasn't held facing the ball, I would look away or even wander off. I didn't get it. Mom and Papa were told to roll the ball toward me. If I didn't react, they were supposed to put the ball in my hands and help me hold on to it, then to react with loud praise as though I had caught it myself.

The positive reinforcement, the psychologists said, would eventually work backward. In the end, I, myself, would want to play catch.

Papa has told me this was a scary time for Mom and him. It was a time when they understood that they'd been fooled—or had been fooling themselves—into believing I was a normal kid who happened to have a rich inner life. When they let themselves see that I wasn't going to be okay unless they burst my bubble, they had to change the whole way they thought about raising kids. They couldn't sit back and let me be me. They had to interfere. It sounded horrible. Violent.

Papa said that the therapists turned out to be right about what they called "physical prompting." He'd been skeptical about moving my body into position like a puppet's. But it worked. I learned very fast to throw and catch the ball and to point in *Goodnight Moon* to the mittens, the socks, the toy house, and the little mouse, instead of staring into space, reciting the rhyming words like music.

Papa said I finally began to look at him for more than a few seconds at a time. He has talked a lot about my early years. Explaining it all to me helps him. I've always tried to understand what he means and then to repeat it back to him.

It's hard to figure out which memories are Papa's and which are mine, but I do have one clear and happy memory of standing in a small circle in our living room, with Papa, Mom, and Elisabeth, passing a ball. Everyone is saying "Bravo" to everyone else. It's great.

Now I'm pretty good at tennis. And softball, basketball, and volleyball. Nothing special, but I'm never the last one to get picked for the team.

Another thing that they told Mom and Papa to do was

to take me to swimming classes. They said it would be good for my self-awareness if I learned to follow directions with my body. And a pool, where I couldn't run away and had to give in to being held and having my body moved in time to the teacher's directions, was the perfect place for me to get started. Mom couldn't take me to swim class because of her career, but Papa was already working at home by then—he was managing money, part-time, for a fund—so that he could be there for me. He took me to the swimming lessons, which were a big success. Even if, according to Papa, the first thing I did was memorize the songs—"The Engine on the Bus Goes Splash Splash Splash" and "Everybody Do the Monkey in the Swimming Pool"—the classes worked.

Now I swim with a team for normal kids, although I avoid swim meets because of the commotion (all those loud whistles and strangers' bodies). Swimming keeps me fit. Not that I'm super muscular, but I'm not as skinny as the French Giotto boys. I think Gilberte has noticed.

Gilberte's very brown eyes were on me when I pulled myself up out of the water after my laps. They grazed my back, the same as in the hawthorns. This time, she was still there when I turned around. I lit up inside.

I had done about a kilometer in the pool. Not far, but enough to steady my nerves. I lay my towel near Simon's and Gilberte's. My towel was light blue. His was gray with white stripes and hers was yellow with big purple stars.

"You're a good swimmer," Marianne said from two towels away. Her hair covered half her face like a dark sheet. "Can I take a picture of you?"

"Sure."

Marianne stood up and pointed her phone at me. The other kids nodded and mumbled that yeah, this American can swim. Kevin popped a Coke can.

"Thanks," I said. "I swim on a team at home, in the States."

"So, is it true," Simon asked, "that Peter Bird is leaving already? He must have a small part?"

"Yeah, he goes next week," I said. "He doesn't have that many scenes. So, they can shoot them all in a few days."

"You mean, they don't shoot the scenes in order?" asked Marianne.

"No, you idiot," said Simon. Then he changed his tone to ask me another question. "He plays Henri II, right?"

"Yeah," Gilberte chimed in. "My dad saw him dying in the Green Garden yesterday. Well, not really dying, but staggering around from his wounds. I guess he was about to die. Dad said it was cool."

"Your dad was at Chenonceau yesterday?" I asked, too loudly. I couldn't help it.

"He works there," she said. "Both my parents do. They're gardeners."

"That's where they plant? At the castle? At Chenonceau? That's incredible!" I yelled.

Everyone laughed except me.

"Why is this incredible to you?" Simon finally asked. "A lot of people's families work at the château. It's boring. *You're* the one whose family is doing something that's interesting." He tried to make eye contact with me. I was almost able to meet him. "By the way," he said, "we were wondering if there is going to be any kind of party when Peter leaves? Have you heard about anything going on for him?"

Moth wings were beating around me, but I didn't care. These kids were cool. And they were talking to me. "I'm sure my mom will plan something. Maybe it will even be at our place. If it's at our place, do you want to come?"

There was silence from the towels. I figured they weren't interested in something as unglamorous as dinner on our terrace. But then, when Simon spoke for the group, I heard nervous excitement. "Yeah, sure, we'll come," he said. Then he added, "And, by the way, I'm having a party at my place a week from Saturday. You'll come, right? My mom is leaving town with my brother, and my dad is never here."

I did not ask why his dad is never here, because I know he is in jail. But then Simon said, "My dad's a trucker. He's always on the road."

I did not contradict him. All I said was "My dad's not around either."

Simon did not get angry. "So, you'll come?" he asked.

"Sure, I'll come to your party," I said.

"Okay, good," said Simon.

Gilberte asked if I wanted to go to the snack bar with her. I said that would be great.

In line, I told her, looking right into her freckled face, how awesome it is that her parents plant flowers at Chenonceau. I said I would look up the names of the plants there and go see Mom on set tomorrow so that I could check out the gardens.

"Let's be clear," she said. "It's much cooler that your mother is shooting a movie with Baxter Wolff, Fuchsia Davis, and Gloria Seegar than that my parents are planting flowers."

"I disagree," I said.

She laughed. She said Mom's movie was way more

important than her parents digging the same holes and planting the same plants every year. "Your mother makes decisions about how everyone looks in a movie and what everyone does in a scene. My parents put flowers exactly where they are told. It's no big deal what they do."

I would not back down. I said her parents' jobs had "prestige."

She shrugged. "What do you want to eat?" she asked.

"I want a Nutella crêpe, please," I said. "What I mean about your parents is that whatever touches on your life is interesting to me."

She laughed again, this time with what I recognized as discomfort, but I couldn't stop myself. I said I'd be interested in where her father went to the dentist. I'd like to follow her mother around while she shopped. "Don't you see, it's because they get to live with you? That makes them wonderful to me."

"You don't even know me!" As she said it, she came two steps closer so that I could see the pores in her skin. Which must mean that she could see my pores too. Wasn't this knowing each other?

"You're right. I don't know you in a normal way," I said. My breath was brushing up against her face and rustling her damp hair. I loved having her this close. "I feel like I've been friends with you for a long time. That's why I am comfortable inviting you to my house for the party or any time you want to come. Usually it takes me months or years to open up to people. With you, there is no time. I recognized you in the hawthorn bushes from the feel of your eyes."

"The hawthorn bushes? What hawthorn bushes?" Her eyes left my face and started darting all around, like mine when I want to escape.

I stuck to my version of things. "Last week, when you watched me in that patch of hawthorn bushes near where I live. You must have been taking a walk?"

"Oh, yeah, the hawthorn bushes," she mumbled. She looked down at the ground. "So, that's why you're inviting us to the party? Because of when we almost met in the hawthorn bushes?"

"Yeah. Something like that."

She didn't say anything, and I got scared she would run away, so I tried to say something normal.

"Do your parents like their work?" I asked.

She didn't answer right away. Then she took a deep breath. "It's a precise job and they are precise people. So I guess it fits their personalities. The vacation time is good, and the retirement is as good as if they worked for the state. So that's good too, I guess. Mostly, they can be precise, which they like. I wouldn't like it, but they do."

"I appreciate precision very much," I said.

"I'm not sure I do," she said. "It bugs me sometimes, how neat the French gardens are, all those perfect triangles and straight lines of plane trees. It doesn't ever bug you that it's so artificial? It seems old-fashioned and boring."

"I love artifice. I'd much rather have artifice than those pretend fake-natural English Romantic gardens. With a French garden, there is romance."

She interrupted me. "Here are our crêpes."

She let me pay for them.

Hers was filled with *crème de marrons*. Chestnut puree.

I debated asking Gilberte what her last name is, but I didn't. I am putting off the not-Swann-ness of it for a little longer. We sat down on a bench to eat.

Through mouthfuls of my crêpe, which was good, I kept insisting that the gardens of Chenonceau were way more epic than any costume drama full of American actors.

"Okay," she finally said, flapping her crêpe at me. I thought I recognized the exhaustion that I get from Mom and Elisabeth when I've been rambling.

I had an idea to get us out of our rut. "Do you want to hear something pretty?" I asked.

"Sure," she said.

I went to get my iPod from my swim bag. I handed her the right earbud and put the left one in my left ear. She put hers in her right ear and said, "I'm ready."

I started playing my sonata. At the beginning, her eyes moved all around. Then they settled on something high up and distant.

I watched her listen. Gilberte and I were having the same experience, but we were also having different experiences. I don't know her well enough to feel how this music affects her. Maybe I'll never know anyone that well. But I want to try.

After four minutes, she whispered, "This is beautiful. I love violins." Then she did not speak again for the entire twenty-three minutes that remained of the piece.

We ate our crêpes slowly while we listened. She looked at her high place and I looked at her. Thin wires connected us and kept us close.

When it was over, she took out her earbud and handed it to me slowly. Her fingers stayed for a beat in my palm. She said, "Thank you," very softly. Then, louder, she said the music was very familiar, but she couldn't remember where she had heard it. She said she only ever liked classical music if she had heard it before.

I said I was the same way. I almost told her Marcel was too.

I was so happy, I knew it couldn't last, so I said I should get going soon.

She touched my palm again. "Maybe if you are so interested in the gardens at Chenonceau, we could go together sometime?" she said.

I couldn't answer out loud, but I smiled.

# Saturday, June 4
## 11:00 p.m.

Since I learned about Gilberte's parents gardening at Chenonceau, I have been reading about the different gardens. A guidebook I found in the cottage where we are staying calls the château's grounds "a veritable theater of green, covering over 12,000 square meters."

The names of its gardens are glowing in my head. Here is a list: the Green Garden, the Italian Maze, the Garden of Wonders, Diane's Garden, Catherine's Garden.

Here is a list of some of the flowers for the summer planting: petunias, tobacco, Lilliput dahlias, impatiens, verveine, begonias. And here is a list of the trees in the

Green Garden: three plane trees, three blue cedar trees, two magnolias, one Spanish fir tree, one catalpa, one chestnut tree, two Douglas fir trees, two sequoias, one two-hundred-year-old holm oak tree, one white acacia, one black walnut tree.

The fact that Gilberte's parents are gardeners at Chenonceau is the most amazing coincidence. My own mother happens to be filming in the exact place where the people closest to Gilberte spend their days. The chances that Mom and her crew have crossed paths with them are excellent. In fact, they are probably crossing paths a lot because this is the busiest time of year in the gardens. And it's a time when Mom is shooting lots of exterior scenes. Gilberte's mother and father are helping to plant one hundred thirty thousand plants for summer, getting the place ready for tourist season. They couldn't miss work, which barely happens in France, even to take care of a sick baby. I'm hoarding this information like treasure.

Monsieur and Madame Gilberte are so lucky to be inside Gilberte's life. They know the details that escape me because I only get to see her in glimpses. I picture Gilberte's father high on a ladder, pruning the acacia. Her mother is planting petunias in a bed. Her parents are historical figures in the garden, as real as Diane de

Poitiers, Henri II, and Catherine de Médicis. It's like I've read a series of books on them and am fascinated by every fact I can find out about their lives. Nothing is too small.

Now my family has a connection to Gilberte's family. I have a real chance to become an *intime*. I can go to Chenonceau any time I want, in order to spot her parents, without looking like I have a weird motive. I have a perfect excuse: my mom is directing a movie there. I can roam the place. I can brush up against Gilberte's parents, say hello, ask them about the flowers, then start a conversation about Gilberte and what she eats for breakfast and what they talk about at home.

This is what it's like to be a moth.

I texted Mom at work today to ask if there is going to be a party at our house for Peter Bird before he takes off.

She texted back, **Let's do something mellow for Peter, at home. Would you want to cook?**

**Sure.**

**What will you make?**

**Fish soup,** I answered. **Can I invite some friends?**

**OF COURSE!**

# Sunday, June 5
## 3:40 p.m.

I don't want to talk about my dream, but I will mention it. I've been dreaming about Gilberte for two years. Now that she's real, the dreams are stronger. This one involved the pool and the towels.

The dream made me upset because it gave me the feeling that I wanted something different from what Gilberte wanted, and that I was pushing her around. I felt violent in a way that isn't me. At least not when I'm awake.

I called Maeva as soon as it was late enough. I told her I'd had an upsetting dream about Gilberte. She said you can't control dreams.

I said I knew that, but what if my dreams are showing that there's something wrong?

She didn't ask me to tell her the dream. She asked what was going on with Gilberte in real life.

I told her about the pool and the gardening and about sharing the sonata. This made me feel better because I realized how different reality is from what I was picturing. While I was talking, I felt the way I did when we were Skyping with the life-skills group. Like I was already a different version of me from the Martin who called Maeva up in a panic.

I told her thank you.

She said to try not to be too literal-minded about my dreams.

I hung up. I started thinking. Even though we seem out of touch with reality, Layla and I are both what they call literal-minded. But we are literal-minded about stories that aren't real, and this can be confusing. It would seem more logical to people if we were excellent at math, for example. But we are not especially good at math. The only way I can put it is this: we take our stories literally.

The best way for me to explain is to give an example from Layla's life. This is how she came to grips with Matthew's death.

When Layla first saw the images of Matthew after his car accident, things made no sense.

After a few seconds, she could decode the blood, the glazed-over eyes, and the body on the side of the country lane as "dead Matthew." She saw it all too large to understand how it fit the plot of *Downton Abbey*. She had an insect's view of the scene. Way too much detail. No perspective. It was upsetting because she loved Matthew. She got that what was happening was bad, but she didn't understand what it meant. She told me there was a rush of red behind her eyes along with confusion. Would Matthew vanish now? It took going over all that had happened leading into the scene for her to see that there was "tragic irony" here. There was tragic irony because Matthew had just come from seeing his wife and newborn baby son, and over the past year he had survived World War I. He'd miraculously recovered from an injury that had almost left him paralyzed. So his death was a cruel twist of fate. For us to understand this took a lot of time and concentration. It was not automatic at all.

The next level of understanding for Layla to work through was this: she learned from fan sites that the actor who played Matthew, Dan Stevens, wanted to be off the show to "pursue other projects." He had a part in a movie called *Summer in February*. He apologized to his upset fans for dying on them so suddenly.

When Layla read this on the internet, she recognized a pattern: other actors make this same choice once they get famous on TV. For example, the actress who played Sybil, the youngest of *Downton*'s three sisters, Jessica Brown Findlay in real life, also decided to pursue Hollywood projects, and so she also died on the show. She died while she was having a baby. This is called "killing off" a character. It happens because an actor wants to leave a show or because a show wants to fire an actor. Regular people know all this without even realizing it. It is second nature. Layla had to learn about killing off characters from the inside out. And then she had to teach it to me.

Now I'm trying to teach myself not to believe my dream of doing things to Gilberte with towels at the pool while she is wearing her white bikini. It's all just images. Like TV.

# Monday, June 6
## 7:20 p.m.

School is less uncomfortable. It's happening in fast-forward.

I don't participate in class, but none of the French kids do either. Teachers here don't care what students think. Students in France are supposed to absorb information, not experiment with self-expression. Which suits me fine. Besides, since I'm sending in my work to The Center, I'm not doing any actual work in the *lycée*. I don't hand in papers or take tests or get grades. I'm only going along for the ride. I sometimes do my Center work during class, but mostly I try to soak in all the French. I mean, French the way people actually speak it these days, not a hundred years ago. Concentrating on following subjects in another language gives me a distance that I like. Translation is a perfect buffer for a kid like me. The force field between French and English. It protects me.

At first, I was a shadow presence in school. I'm getting more solid now. I have my little lunch crowd that I sit with. There are six kids I say hi to regularly in the yard and the hallways. And I'm not only saying hi to their shoes anymore. I wouldn't call myself "adjusted," but I would say that I am getting used to general-ed. None of it seems quite so drastic.

Layla doesn't seem happy about this. Today, when I texted her about the party at our house for Peter and told her that my friends are going to come, she texted back: **Beware of moths.**

I answered: **They may be moths, but they are also friends. Like you are a moth and a friend.**

**It is rare to be both.**

**How can you be sure?**

**Do you think our phones are instruments of communication or torture?**

Before I could text her back again, Layla called me. I stared at the ringing phone in disbelief. Even Layla and I get that teenagers don't talk on the phone. Our life is epistolary. So the ringing, with a close-up of her big green eyes and clumpy lashes filling up my screen, was totally weird.

I answered.

"Layla, what's up?" I tried to sound casual.

"Please, don't get all neurotypical on me, Martin. I'm worried about you. I'm calling to warn you. They are moths, Martin, and not friends. They only want you around because of who your mom is. They are probably laughing at you behind your back."

I could picture her curled up on the enormous brown suede sofa facing the giant screen in her basement. She looked very small, and she was kneading her big hands together the way she does when she is anxious, so that her knuckles went up and down uncontrollably, like waves.

I wanted to make her okay.

"Yes, Layla, they are technically moths. But that's not all there is. Stuff is different here. I'm starting to understand more things."

"How is it"—her voice cracked—"that you can't see? What about all the deceit you have learned about in *Search*? You should know you can't always trust people."

This made me angry. "You haven't even read *Search*," I said. As soon as I said it I wasn't angry anymore, only sad. I'm in the beautiful French countryside, while she is stuck in her lonely basement in LA.

Layla says that I am the only family she has, along with Maeva at The Center, and sometimes Lady Grantham. Technically, this is not true because Layla has her parents, both of them together, along with two typically developing older sisters. Her parents and sisters let her do whatever she wants. They barely interfere, except to hire people to help her. She has overheard them say that they are throwing money at the problem.

When she didn't respond to my comment about her not reading *Search*, I said, "I'm sorry."

"Okay. Just please don't disappear on me. Don't pull a Michael Gregson."

She wanted me to ask her who Michael Gregson was. So I did. "Who is Michael Gregson?"

"Please don't do to us at The Center what Michael Gregson has done to Edith."

I figured that Michael Gregson was a character from *Downton Abbey*. "What has Michael done to Edith? You haven't given me that plot line yet."

"Let's say there's potential for abandonment."

"Abandonment? I'm not going to abandon you."

Suddenly, I was with her in her basement, even though I was physically pacing up and down on the grass between the cottage and the pool. The grass is full of dandelions. Their softness started to remind me of the softness of her couch, which you sink into, like a furry marshmallow. At first this was a good feeling of being next to my best friend. But after a few minutes of her telling me about Edith and Michael and how Edith found out she was pregnant while she still had no idea where Michael was, and going into more and more detail, I was trapped in a dark place where I didn't want to be. The brown sofa was sucking me in.

I interrupted her. "I'm not disappearing like Michael Gregson. Or like anyone else. I'm not disappearing from you or from The Center. I'll be home in a month. I promise."

"You're not being a good listener, Martin," she said, sadly.

"You're not being a good listener either. You don't trust me when I say I'm not going to abandon my roots." I was Odette, defending myself to Mr. Swann, who thought I was lying. Which meant that Layla was acting like the jealous one. Was Layla jealous? "I'm thinking of going to a party. That's all. Nothing has changed."

"I thought they were coming to *your* party for Peter Bird."

I did not want her to react this way. I also did not want

to lie to her. Because if I lied to her, then it would be logical for her to be jealous. "They are coming to our party for Peter. Then, next weekend, I might go to a party at Simon's house while his mom is out of town."

"Is that wise? I think I need to hang up."

"Thanks for calling, Layla."

"Bye."

"Bye."

After we hung up, I picked seven dandelions and blew them all away.

# Tuesday, June 7
## 5:50 p.m.

Every time Mom catches my eye, she smiles. She is happy that I have friends to invite to our party.

If Papa could see, he would say that I was becoming a real artisan. An artisan is someone who makes things on his own instead of repeating.

I used to spout entire books, songs, and phrases copied from adults. When speech is repetitive, it's perfect. There is no mess. It's the cake thing: all the ingredients measured and lined up on the kitchen counter, waiting.

The experts told my parents I had no original speech. That if I ever did start to really speak, I wouldn't speak perfectly anymore, but in mashed-together phrases that could be called "artisanal" because they would be home-made. If I started to sound like a small child or some-one speaking a foreign language, this would be a great sign. It might seem like I was sliding backward, talking baby talk. In fact, the goofy speech would be the begin-ning of the real me.

Papa latched on to the word *artisanal*.

If he asked me, "Do you want to do the puzzle of the cow?" and I answered, "You don't want to do the puzzle of the cow," he tried to argue that I was saying something of my very own. Dad is an optimist.

Mom wasn't buying it. She said that when I said I didn't want to do the puzzle, I was echoing Papa, in the negative. I hadn't changed one word of his question. She said he needed to face this.

"No," Papa said. "These negations of Martin's are orig-inal speech. They're artisanal."

"What is it with the artisanal? You're making Martin sound like a cheese or a vinegar."

Papa kept the faith. Maybe cheese and vinegar weren't such bad things. He called me his "young artisan" with affection in his voice. The last words he said to me be-fore he had to go to jail were, "I believe in you, young ar-tisan. Always remember I love you and I believe in you."

# Wednesday, June 8
## 9:35 p.m.

Years from now, when this afternoon has become hopelessly out of date, it won't seem at all hopeless to Gilberte and me.

I wanted to ask her to meet me after school at the *boulangerie* in town. Three times, I tried to say something. I tried in the hallway between math and history. I tried in the cafeteria. I tried right after the bell rang at the end of chemistry. All three times, I said, "I would like to ask you something." The first time, she smiled and asked, "What?" I couldn't respond. The second time, she laughed, then asked, "What is it, Martin?" I still couldn't respond. The third time, she didn't smile or laugh. She said, "If you don't tell me what it is, I can't answer." I just stood there in the door of the classroom until somebody said "Excuse me" and I had to move.

There was a fourth time. It was in the yard, at the end of school, and it was my last chance. I saw her ponytail and her gladiator sandals, and I ran after them. I had to change my opening line or I was going to get stuck again. So instead of "I would like to ask you something," I said, "Do you like madeleines?"

"Yes," she said. "Do you?"

"Yes," I said. "Do you want to get some right now?"

She looked down at her toes. I thought she was annoyed at me. Then she looked up and said, "Yes."

We went into the *boulangerie* together. I bought a bag of six madeleines. Because I was with Gilberte, I had no trouble asking the lady in the pink apron for what I wanted. I paid without any problem. Gilberte picked an Orangina to drink. I got myself iced tea because there was no hot tea for sale, which was quite flexible of me.

We sat on a bench in a small shady square. At first, I didn't open the madeleines. The scalloped ridges through the paper bag made me smile.

She asked me about my hand-painted sneakers. "Why are there butterflies on your shoes?"

"They are moths. My friend Layla back in California painted them."

She arched her eyebrows. "Is Layla your girlfriend?"

"Of course not."

"Why does she paint moths?"

"Moths are the people who flutter around the glamour of my mom's movies. The big fans and the fascinated people. The ones who really hang on."

"So you don't like the moths." She frowned.

"No, that's not it. Not all moths are bad. Layla is good, and she's a moth herself. 'I am a moth drawn to the flame of glamour.' That's what she says. She copies them from insect books."

I looked down at my Converses, then back up at Gilberte. She had her hair pulled into a ponytail like on the first day we spoke. She had even more freckles than before. She was still frowning, but not a sad frown. I recognized puzzlement. She reminded me of when I'm trying to work out something that might be important.

I wanted to tell her again how amazing it was for me to be able to look straight at her without even flinching, but I didn't want to seem weird.

Also, Elisabeth gave me some advice this morning to prep me for seeing Gilberte: "Remember, it's not all about you and your perceptions. Make it about her too."

145

I want to follow Elisabeth's advice. Only I have no model for this kind of back and forth, because the love in *Search* is all one-sided.

I start trying to think of questions to ask Gilberte about herself. But all my questions—about her past, her parents, her habits—are what Maeva calls obsessive and inappropriate. I can't ask a single one.

I begin to stress out. I'm sweating. I'm scared I am going to groan. My guts stretch into taut violin strings. I have no idea how to loosen them except to make horrible yowls. The groaning is coming on. I grab the bench with one hand. The other hand is gripping the madeleine bag. I stop myself from rocking, but I won't be able to hold back for long.

I'm about to ruin everything, when she rescues me. She brushes her hand over mine and says, "Are we going to eat our cakes or what?"

"Yeah, we are." Miraculously, my voice is steady, but it's a disconnected, underwater voice.

"Okay then, let's go!"

Slowly, I open the bag, hand her a madeleine, and take one myself. I am with Gilberte eating Proust's madeleines. I wait for fireworks to begin bursting in my chest. What happens is that my heartbeat slows down to normal. For a few seconds, I'm as calm as I've ever been. The leafy square around us comes into focus.

The first madeleine tastes good.

"These are famous from Proust," she says.

"You've read Proust?" I whisper. I start to tingle. I brush the top of her hand the way she brushed mine a few moments ago, and I touch the tiny soft hairs on her skin. Then I rest my hand on top of hers. When I do this, I think time might stop. Only it doesn't and she keeps on talking.

While she is talking, she turns her hand over so that our palms touch and our fingers interlock. It's so much better than any dream.

This is what she is saying: "In France, everyone has to read passages of Proust. You can't escape. It's part of our culture. Even if you don't 'know' it, you have to have some idea. I've only read that first section about when he eats the madeleine and remembers stuff. And then I saw a super-boring movie once about a guy named Swann who was obsessed with some woman."

"Wow." She's talking about *Search*. She's holding my hand for real. The groaning is gone. I smile at her.

"You've read Proust?" she asks me.

"I have read it a few times," I answer, "but only the first volume."

"That's bizarre for an American, no? To read a French author."

"My dad is French."

"Oh, right, I forgot."

"Maybe this seems bizarre for a kid my age?"

"No, no. It's not bizarre," she says. "It's different. I don't know very many different people."

"So different is good?"

"Yeah. It makes people curious. Like your music at the pool. No one else plays violin music like that. It makes me want to know you."

She moves her hand and resettles her fingers around mine. This is fun. Holding hands seems almost normal. I've never adjusted to anything this fast.

She asks if school is different in America. I admit that I don't attend the most typical school, so I might not be the best person to answer her question. I tell her that in most schools in America, kids are encouraged to express themselves and ask lots of questions. This is supposed to be good for critical thinking, although you could argue that it also wastes a lot of everyone's time.

She nods.

Then she asks about how Mom's movie is going, and her fingers start to wriggle in my grip. They are like wings beating against glass. She glances at my sneakers. Could she be nervous? I don't want her to be nervous.

Making my voice calm, I tell her that the movie is going well and that we should go check out a shoot together. Maybe we can go when they are doing one of the crowd scenes that Simon will be in? I say I really want to go on set at Chenonceau to see her parents gardening, like we talked about at the pool. When she laughs at this, I am happy.

She lets go of my hand to take another madeleine.

We ate all six. Three each. I told her that I've always thought that the experience of eating madeleines in France would have to somehow stick to the book, like a blueprint. I said I'd never been able to picture just how this perfect symmetry would happen, because I am not exactly an old man trying to recapture my life.

I could see that she wasn't following what I was saying. Her eyes were moving all around the square, and she was peeling the label off her Orangina bottle with her fingernails. They were painted green. She had something else on her mind besides madeleines. Something that had nothing to do with Proust. I recognized this because I have watched Layla when her mind is so full of music that she doesn't see the world around her.

Gilberte was in her own bubble.

We sat for a while without talking.

At some point, I asked her if she liked white hawthorns or pink hawthorns better. I tried not to care about her answer, but pink hawthorns are rarer and more exciting to Marcel, so it was hard not to hope.

Her gaze went down again. "Listen, when you said you saw me in the hawthorn bushes—"

"I didn't see you!" I said too loudly. "You saw me."

It's very hard for me not to correct inaccuracies. I was overdoing it, but she seemed to forgive me because she looked back up at me and she smiled. A little sadly, but she smiled.

"Well, I should get going," she said.

When we were saying good-bye, she asked, "So, day after tomorrow?" I heard shyness, which made me think that she was nervous about saying she wanted to see me again soon.

"Of course."

"You sure it's cool if we all come to the party? Your mom doesn't mind?"

"Very cool. It's only dinner on our terrace at the little

house we've rented. Nothing fancy. My mom is fine with it."

I almost told Gilberte that my mom can hardly believe I have friends and is so psyched you're all coming that she's pinching herself to make sure she isn't dreaming.

# Thursday, June 9
## 10:35 p.m.

Asparagus Man had the nerve to tell me at breakfast that I was acting like a crazy man in a book called *Don Quixote*. I told him that was impossible because I've never even read *Don Quixote*, so I can't be copying him. Asparagus Man laughed and said it didn't matter. He told me Don Quixote was a type. Don Quixote believed he was an errant knight from out of his books of chivalry, and he wasted his life defending the honor of a woman he didn't even know. She was some milkmaid he had "elevated in his fantasy." Asparagus Man said I too am trying to live according to some code in an outdated book.

I can't stand him.

I wished Layla was here to stun him with a quote from Lady Grantham or play the first few bars of "Paint It Black." But I was on my own. I also wished I hadn't told everyone at dinner last night about spending the afternoon with Gilberte eating madeleines. It was none of his business. He should never have been there at our dinner, scarfing our goat cheese with our lavender honey, listening to our conversation. With his *Don Quixote* thing, he was trying to be my pal by acting literary. I wasn't biting.

I wanted to say to him that he didn't get it, that at first I loved Gilberte because of Proust, but now I loved Proust because of Gilberte. I didn't say anything.

Asparagus Man asked me if I was cooking for Peter's dinner tomorrow night.

I did not want to answer, but I have been taught through years of behavioral therapy not to leave a question hanging.

I said that I had been planning to make fish soup, but it now seemed too hot for soup, so I was making a tomato-and-olive salad and a green-bean-and-shallot salad. Mom is ordering cold poached salmon and roast chickens from the *traiteur* in town.

He seemed satisfied and left me alone.

The food at the party is going to be delicious.

Bernadette is making clafoutis for dessert, which is a kind of flan with fresh cherries. In France, they don't take the pits out. Mom has asked Bernadette to pit the cherries for the Americans, otherwise there is sure to be some drama, like a broken tooth or swallowed pits or choking. Bernadette says this is ridiculous, and my guess is that she will leave some of the cherries intact to show us who is boss.

When I met Bernadette, I asked her if she had ever wrung the neck of a chicken because I'd read in a French novel about a cook named Françoise chasing a chicken around a yard and calling it a "dirty beast." I wondered if this still happened in real life. She twisted together her own gnarly hands. Then she told me that her father used to wring the necks of chickens, ducks, and geese, and that she had watched him. Even though she had never done it herself, she had a good idea how it must feel. "The idea does not shock me at all," she said. This was good enough for me.

# Friday, June 10
## 4:50 p.m.

This is the note, written on lined paper ripped out of a spiral notebook, that Gilberte handed me at school this morning.

Hey Martin,

    We are not coming to your party tonight. At least I'm not. We are assholes. We are using you like the glamour moths your friend draws on your shoes, okay? You need to understand this. We've all been treating you like a fool, lying to you about wanting to be your friends, but I'm the worst one because I could tell that you liked me and I led you on. I never saw you in any hawthorn bushes. I have no idea what you are talking about a lot of the time. My name is not Gilberte. I didn't correct you when you said these things because I wanted to meet movie stars and to help Simon get into the scenes he wanted to get into because he's upset about his dad and he has all these dreams. So we are users. We don't deserve your trust. Everyone will be mad at me for writing this, but they should also be ashamed because you are a nice, trusting guy. Anyway, I'm not going through with it. And I doubt the others will now either.

Alice

P.S. I wrote a letter by hand because I didn't want anything floating around online. Also, you seem like the kind of person who would want a handwritten note because you are so connected to the past.

I was in a bathroom stall when I read this letter. Here is how I responded: I screamed "Fuck!" eight times. I was sure screaming "Fuck" would break my tension, but I was wrong because right after I was done screaming I started to rock and to groan loudly. I didn't want to be groaning in a bathroom stall. So I stopped myself by yelling "Fuck" again, ten times. Then I threw up. I had eaten mostly apricots for breakfast. The vomit was orange.

I texted Elisabeth to come get me right away.

**Are you okay?** she texted back immediately.

**No.** Then I took a Sharpie out of my backpack and wrote FUCK on the stall door. I felt better. FUCK, I wrote again.

So this was original speech.

A moment later, staring at my graffiti, I realized it wasn't original at all.

When I said the word *fuck*, I was imitating Elisabeth when she stubs her toe or slices her finger in the kitchen. I wasn't saying anything new.

I burst out laughing. Too loudly. Papa was right, there's no such thing as original speech. It's a sham idea. A joke. I laughed louder.

I finally stopped and came out of the stall. If there had been anyone in the bathroom, I had scared them away with my groaning, puking, and laughing. It was empty.

I rinsed out my mouth and splashed water on my face.

I looked in the mirror, wishing I could be weirder looking so that I wouldn't keep disappointing people. People get fooled by what Mom calls my "sweet, handsome face" into expecting sweet, handsome behavior. Then I freak them out. Not that I want to. I don't like to be scared, so why would I choose to be scary?

My scariness would probably be easier to take if it was more visible, like if I was deformed or ugly. Then again, if I was ugly, Gilberte—or Alice—wouldn't have been able to pretend she liked me, and I never would have been happy.

Even when you're disappointing, you can still be disappointed.

Of all the faces on the emotion work sheets the teachers at The Center gave me when I was little to help me learn to recognize feelings, disappointed was the best fit. There was sad, happy, worried, angry, excited, and disappointed.

I really thought she liked me. The way she tickled my palm when she returned my earbud. The way she smiled when she said she would meet me at the bakery. The way she settled her hand in mine on the bench like a small animal getting cozy. The way she raised her eyebrows when she asked if Layla was my girlfriend. They say when you raise your eyebrows you are showing concern. But I guess I read her all wrong.

I put on my headphones to block out images of what I had just lost. Falling into the sound was like sinking into a pool of cotton balls. I was able to lose my train of thought.

But not for long.

Usually, once the music starts, there's nothing else. No bathroom mirror. No note from my "friend." Only sound. But today, even with the music playing, I could not stop thinking about the letter or forget where I was.

I texted Elisabeth to hurry, that I would be waiting on the street.

**Are you sure you want to leave school this early?** she wrote back.

**Yes, I'm sure.** I typed to the rhythm of the piano.

For the first time in my life, I was multitasking! Welcome to your generation, Martin.

When Elisabeth pulled up, I was in the middle of the second movement of my sonata. I asked her if it was okay if I kept my headphones on until it finished.

"Sure," she said. "It's really cool of you to ask if I mind. You've never asked that before." After that, she drove and did not talk until my movement was over and I took the headphones off. Then she asked, "Do you feel okay now?"

"Not really."

"Do you want to go home or drive into town? Or do you want to go find Mom on set? They're shooting in the rose garden today. Arthur says it's beautiful."

"No, thanks. Let's go home. I think the gardens might make me sad today."

"What happened?"

"I'm disappointed. I don't know if I can explain. But I have a question."

"Shoot."

"Am I a fool?"

"Who called you a fool?" She sped up around a narrow curve and the Smart car brushed against a lilac bush. There was a scratching sound. I felt the scratching behind my eyes. I did not want Elisabeth to feel sorry for me. I started to cry. "You're not a fool," she said.

"But I am easy to trick."

"I don't think you're easy to trick," she said. "That's not it at all. I do think you have a really strong picture of your world in your head, and it can be very different from other people's pictures. They might think you're naïve and that they are making fun of you, but what you are is original. That can seem foolish to people who aren't used to it. You can't entirely blame them."

I didn't respond to Elisabeth. What I did was take her final sentence—"You can't entirely blame them"—and say it over and over in my head. I kept repeating it silently at the cottage while I changed into my swim trunks, dove into our pool, which Mom does not believe in heating, and started going back and forth. Our pool is only four strokes long, but I did not get frustrated about the quick turns because my mind was also turning quickly inside. "You can't entirely blame them, you can't entirely blame them, you can't entirely blame them . . ." With the rhythm of the words and the strokes, I was able to think.

Here is what I thought: Gilberte/Alice wrote me a letter. Even if it is a terrible letter, she did get one thing right: I enjoy handwritten letters on real paper. At least she's been paying attention. And even if she is deceitful, I still want her near me. But I don't think she's deceitful. I think maybe I didn't look at her clearly enough to see how she felt.

I'm disappointed, but I guess I should get used to the way kids act. If I was as general-ed as Simon, Gilberte/Alice, and their friends, and if I lived someplace where not a lot new happens and people are mostly excited about smoking and Renaissance history, I would probably be a moth to the flame of movie glamour too. I would tell lies to get myself invited to a movie-star party.

I stopped swimming and looked up at the sky. I counted five birds, very high up. Then I saw a sixth one. The more I looked, the more birds I saw. My body standing still in the cool water was muscular. My eyes were strong enough to count a thousand birds.

I am not a fool and the moths are not assholes.

I wished I could call Maeva or text Layla to tell them what I planned to do next, but it was 2:30 a.m. in Los Angeles. I had to believe that they would support me. But I also had to make my decision on my own.

I did not want to take more time away from Elisabeth's work. So I got dressed and walked all the way back to school to find the moths. It wouldn't be a party without them.

# Saturday, June 11
## 10:50 a.m.

There's a postcard taped to my wall. It's a painting of an erupting volcano. I look at it when things are rough. It's called *The Eruption of Mount Vesuvius*. It's by an English Romantic painter named J. M. W. Turner. It looks across a fiery bay to the exploding mountain. There are boats getting tossed around and there is a crowd of people staring up from the beach. Compared to the volcano, the people are tiny, but they are still very detailed.

I am guessing that this painting was one of Marcel's favorites, because it's both scary and totally awesome at the same time. It brings me huge relief. If the volcano rocks and groans for me when I stare at it, then I don't have to do it myself.

Marcel's grandmother wanted to fill his room at Combray with images of beautiful sites and scenes from history. She was scared photographs would be "vulgar" because they were too "utilitarian." So she asked Mr. Swann to help her find photographs of paintings of the sites and scenes. She thought this would avoid "commercial banality." In this way, she gave Marcel several "thicknesses," or layers, of art: the original, the painting, and the photograph of the painting.

In my postcard collection, I have two of the pictures that Marcel's grandmother gave to him: Corot's *Chartres Cathedral* and Turner's *Vesuvius*. They're both on my wall here.

After I got home from school yesterday, I stared at the Turner volcano for forty-five minutes, tracing the lava flows with my finger. Mom knocked on my door. So did Elisabeth. They asked if I was okay. I told them I was busy.

Mom knocked again. She asked, did I remember that people are coming at 7:30 p.m.?

Of course I remembered. What a stupid question. I have a painfully accurate memory. Mom, of all people, should know this. I did not tell her she was being illogical because I have learned that, when people get worried or anxious, they ask stupid questions, and it's mean to call them on it. So instead of saying, "Why would you ask me that?" I said, "I'm busy," again, which was true. I was busy going over what happened with the moths.

Walking down the big hill to town, I had texted Simon and Gilberte/Alice to meet me right after school under the basketball hoop in the yard, but I hadn't texted back when they asked why.

They had both shown up. They looked down at their feet while I told them I wanted them to come to the party even if they were using me.

The weird thing was that while I was waiting for them to come to the basketball court, I was trembling. I thought I might throw up again. But when I saw how nervous they were, staring at their shoes like I usually do, I started talking fast in order to make them less uncomfortable. I stopped shaking.

I told them that I was used to people wanting to hang out with me because of Mom. I told them about Layla being a moth like them, only not as normal. And I explained that people usually become attached to other people for very weird reasons (think Mr. Swann and Odette) and that it probably wasn't worth getting upset about. I didn't care if they liked me at first because of who my mother is. It was a doorway into somewhere

165

else. Eventually, if we become friends, they might realize they like Mom *because* she is related to me instead of wanting to be friends with me because she's famous.

They ended up laughing. It was a relief.

I never imagined I would be able to make general-ed kids feel better about themselves. It's like all the practicing I've done at The Center has translated into this new world. I took a lifeguarding course once, and I always wondered if the techniques you used on the dummies would work on real people. Now I know.

After our conversation in the yard, I was okay.

When I got home, I got shaky again. So I went into my room to stare at the volcano postcard. Suddenly it seemed crazy to have invited the kids from school to this party with my family and Mom's cast and crew. How the hell was *I* going to manage to connect such different groups? It was going to be noisy, confusing, and stressful. What had I taken on?

"Are you freaking out in there?" Elisabeth asked through my door. "Don't worry. We're not going to bite your friends."

"I'm busy," was all I could say.

The person who finally got me out was Bernadette. She did it by threatening about my salads. She said that if I did not slice, seed, and salt my tomatoes soon, they would not have time to drain in the colanders I had set up, and then my salad—tomatoes, olives, red onion, chevre, parsley, olive oil—would be soggy. This would be a "desecration." Bernadette also reminded me that she had prepped three kilos of green beans for me, which was hours of work. If I did not come downstairs and blanch them soon, her work would be wasted. The beans would not cool in time for the vinaigrette.

My awe of Bernadette is like Marcel's awe of Françoise, the family cook. It's not rational, but it's powerful. I stopped staring at Vesuvius, got up, and headed downstairs to work.

While I was cooking, I was able to focus on my tasks and stop worrying about how the party was going to be. Papa says that work is the best distraction.

They all came: Gilberte/Alice, Simon, Marianne, and the Giotto-chested boys. They came riding double on mopeds. Simon brought a bottle of rosé in a bag from his mom's supermarket, Intermarché. Mom said, *"Merci."*

It was happening the way weather happens. Breaking like a storm. I wanted to run upstairs, but I didn't.

I introduced Gilberte as "Alice" to Elisabeth and to Mom. They say pretending to believe in reality is the first step to belonging there. But it can be confusing. I didn't sound very convincing, though, because Elisabeth took me aside and said, "Is that *her*? So her actual name is not Gilberte? It's Alice?"

"Well, it is and it isn't," I said quietly. I might as well have spoken out loud because none of the moths can understand English.

"Got it." Elisabeth didn't seem annoyed by my confusion. "Well, whoever she is, she's pretty."

"Yeah, she is. You think she's pretty too. You like her freckles."

"Pronouns," she whispered.

"I mean, *I* like her freckles."

She smiled, squeezed my hand, and spun me out to face the friends or the moths or whatever they are. Then she turned around to give Arthur a kiss. Her top plunged down her back. She made it yesterday out of black silk. She's been sewing a lot since her breakup with Jason and starting to see Arthur. She seems happier. She doesn't act as nervous about her organic chemistry.

The members of the cast and crew were all milling around, drinking, eating olives and anchovies. The kids from school were in their own cluster. My salads were ready on a buffet in the kitchen along with the cold poached salmon and roast chicken, which we were serving room temperature. It wasn't dinnertime yet.

A pair of soft bare arms grabbed me from behind. It's

a good thing I'm not super sensory about being touched, because people can be very invasive.

It was Fuchsia.

"Hey, special one!" She really called me that. "Are these your friends? Aren't you going to introduce me?"

I froze.

She laughed. "Let me help you. 'Guys, this is my friend, Fuchsia. Fuchsia, this is . . .'" Here she gestured to Simon, meaning that this was my cue to insert his name. Then she brushed her fingers against my cheek.

I was grateful to Fuchsia for her prompt. Prompting is a reassuring technique. It's a part of what they call "scaffolding" at The Center. Fuchsia's fingers on my skin while she prompted me reminded me of Papa's thumb caressing my cheek to relax my jaw while he helped me learn to talk. Papa gave me scaffolding all the time.

For example, at breakfast, he might ask: "Would you like eggs or cereal?" When I stared into my napkin instead of answering, he would give me words to build on: "I would like . . ."

At first, I repeated, "I would like eggs or cereal." Finally, one day when I was five, I got it. Papa asked, "Would you like oatmeal or pancakes?" Then he prompted, "I would like . . ." Suddenly, I realized I wanted pancakes. I said, "I would like pancakes! Just pancakes!"

Papa started crying. He said it was because he was happy.

I spent a few moments remembering the pancake morning. I forgot about Fuchsia. So, she prompted me again, which was nice of her. "'Fuchsia,'" she said, "'this is . . .'" and she gestured to Simon a second time.

I kicked in. "Fuchsia," I said, "this is Simon."

"Lovely to meet you, Simon." She held out her hand to him.

He stared at her breasts. Then he forced himself to focus on her face while he shook hands. I have done this myself. "Hello, Fuchsia," he said, with such a strong French accent that I reeled from the difference between his coolness in French and his flailing English.

Then I used Fuchsia's introductory formula again, but this time I grouped all the others together in a list, with "Alice" at the end.

"Great to meet all you guys! Welcome to our party!" Fuchsia was bubbly, like she was demonstrating a positive personality type in one of Maeva's role-playing games. I appreciated her effort.

The kids mostly mumbled something back at Fuchsia in broken English. Except for Gilberte/Alice, who stuck with what she knows, which is usually a good idea. She said, *"Enchantée."*

"*Enchantée*," Fuchsia tossed back. Then she moved on into the crowd.

I'm not so good at gauging other people's comfort levels, except when I recognize my own symptoms in other people. Then I get sensitive. This is called "empathy."

I had empathy with my moth friends at the party because I saw them looking down at their feet a lot, not mingling, eating and drinking furtively, like squirrels. They reminded me of me in unfamiliar groups. This made me ache for them.

They were uncomfortable for two reasons.

1. They were shy with the cast and the movie crew. Fuchsia and Gloria, Baxter and Peter were all mythical beings to them. Seeing your myths in the flesh is overwhelming.
2. People around them were speaking English, which meant they had no idea what was going on.

Here in Mom's world, on our terrace with the film crew, the cool kids from the *lycée* were the ones who were on the outside.

For the first time in my life, I thought I might be a useful guide. Not that I could explain to them what was going on, or who was friends with whom, or what the gossip was. But if there is one thing I can do, it's translate. The space between French and English is my comfort zone. When I translate, I go back and forth; I swim laps, up one side and down the other. I can't think too much or I'll lose the rhythm.

I figured that if I decoded for the moths, they would be okay. It was exciting.

What I did was this: I found the closest conversation that I was comfortable approaching, which was between Mom and Peter. I began translating bits of it in a loud whisper to Gilberte/Alice while the others listened in.

Mom:  "So, you're heading to London?"
Peter:  "I might spend a day or two in Paris first."
Mom:  "Where are you staying?"
Peter:  "Rue Cassette, in the sixth. A friend's place."
Mom:  "Cute street."
Peter:  "You know it?"
Mom:  "My ex-husband grew up in that neighborhood."

When Mom used the term "ex-husband," I got a jolt of nausea. So I moved on to a different conversation.

I figured it didn't matter to the French kids what

people were talking about. The moths don't need substance. All they need is not to be locked out.

We moved away from Mom and Peter on to a small group of camera people, set designers, and grips. I didn't have my usual problem looking at them head-on because I was too busy translating to register fear.

There was a lot of overlapping and interrupting in the crew's speech. I latched on where I could.

"I got this awesome red wine called Chinon at the supermarket in town for like nine euros."

"It's supposed to rain on Tuesday. Sam's going to have to change the schedule. We're supposed to do that big scene with Gloria in the garden."

"My wife has an obsession with this stinky French cheese. She says if I get it vacuum-packed the customs dogs won't be able to smell it."

"That Antoine guy at the castle is kind of an asshole."

"So, wait, which red was it? Because there's like twenty shelves of wine in that market."

"We almost destroyed this ancient canopy bed. I can't believe they let us use it. That thing is irreplaceable. Can you imagine that happening in the States? The insurance they would make you get for all this priceless furniture! And here they let us co-opt it for our shoots."

"Fuck French wine. French wine is so overrated."

Until dinner, the moths and I fluttered around together, eavesdropping. It got us to relax. People smiled at us. Elisabeth explained to me that the French kids were local color for us Americans. "Not only is it awesome that you have made friends and decided to invite them, but it lends a certain je ne sais quoi to Mom's little get-together. It's authentic."

By the time Mom told everyone to grab a plate and fill it in the kitchen, the moths had chilled enough to talk to one another, and to me. We were our own subgroup of *intimes* within the clan. We were taking pictures. It was good.

We sat at a table together to eat. Gilberte/Alice was sitting next to me. I had imagined her eating my string beans. Only I had pictured her picking them up gracefully with her fingers and nibbling them down. In reality, she cut them with a knife and fork and ate them fast. This made me want to hold her.

Mom gave a toast about what a great guy Peter is, how it makes sense that two of history's most powerful women would fight over him. She joked about how she was glad he wasn't really dead from a jousting wound. Then Peter made a toast about how talented Mom is and about how she always has the happiest and best-fed crews, how she creates community.

I translated the toasts for the moths.

Afterward, Gilberte/Alice said that I was so good at translating that she was understanding the words from Mom's and Peter's lips and not from me at all. She used the word *effacé*, which means "erased," to describe me. Then she said something nice but not accurate: "It's kind of you to do this for us. It must be such a pain and such an effort."

Under the table, she put her hand on my knee. To steady myself, I put my hand on top of her hand.

"Translating is automatic," I managed to say through my excitement. "It's not an effort to translate. It's something you do. It helps you feel better too."

"Yeah, well, it helps *you* feel better to be nice. Not everyone. You could be way more of a snob because you know these famous people and this movie world. It's nice of you. That's all."

"Thanks." I moved my hand to her knee and started rubbing it. Her kneecap was perfectly round. Her skin was soft.

She smiled at me. Through my jeans, she began rubbing my knee too. We didn't talk about what we were doing. It just happened under the table, like fronds of seaweed moving together beneath the surface of a stream. Like a whole silent world.

"You'll see," she said, as though nothing incredible was happening to our knees, "the party at Simon's, it won't be this way at all."

"I guess there won't be so many adults at Simon's, right?"

"Right," she agreed. "There won't be *any* adults. And everything will be completely not of the same class. You'll see. I'm glad you're still coming to Simon's. I'm glad we're friends. You . . ." Here she stared at my face, and I managed to stare back, even though I was erupting inside. "You're not normal like other people. French people, they can get very upset when things and people are different."

"You realize this. You've met some of your dad's French relatives!"

I think I squeezed her knee too hard because she clenched her face. So I took my hand away. She rested hers on my thigh and kept it still.

She gave me a confused look. "Didn't you mean to say 'I'? '*I've* met some of *my* dad's French relatives'?"

This was a moment when I could either stammer and drift away or let her in. I let her in.

"My pronouns are sometimes backward when I get anxious," I said. "I start talking through a mirror, where I am you and you are me."

"Weird."

I had blown it. She thought I was weird. Not normal.

Before I could bolt, she went on. "I mean, weird in a very cool way. I don't want things to be normal. It's so boring."

I must have smiled because she smiled back.

Marcel and Gilberte could not have had this moment. His Gilberte was too absorbed in her own world to notice his personality. My Gilberte/Alice saying what she thought of me was a real break from *Search*. This had its problems, but it was worth it.

There was a new kind of buzzing inside me. It did not scare me. It wasn't fear. It was a series of small bursts, like a shoot pushing up through the soil.

Mom clinked her glass and announced that dessert was ready.

At dessert, there were cherry pits in Bernadette's clafoutis. I swallowed six of them and spit out two. None of the French moths seemed to notice. I worried that Mom would be stressed about people choking or breaking teeth. I saw her glance around anxiously at the guests. When, after two minutes, there were no incidents, she visibly relaxed. I was happy, but not surprised, that Bernadette had stuck to her recipe.

When I said good-bye to the moths, Alice kissed me on both cheeks and then for a second on the lips. Marcel would have been desperate for this moment never to end. But I felt something else. I was astonished that life didn't freeze. The party kept going on even though the greatest thing ever was happening to me.

The moths headed away from our cottage on their mopeds, making a noise like my flies. Only instead of going into themes and variations, the mopeds' buzzing faded quickly into the night.

Mom had hired two women from the café in the village to help serve and clean up. They were clearing plates. The clanking was musical. Most everyone was gone by now. Asparagus Man was lingering in the kitchen.

Mom put her arm around me.

"Nice friends you've made." She sounded hopeful and tired.

# Sunday, June 12
## 6:40 p.m.

How was the party? Layla wrote today. How did the neurotypical moths behave?

My regrets were calmed. I let myself give in to the sweetness of the night.

Don't be nostalgic, dear. It's very middle class.

She was quoting Lady Grantham and I was quoting Marcel. We are both quoting now, I wrote. That's why we're friends.

Are we? Are you sure? How are we friends these days?

Of course I am sure. Are you angry because I had my moth friends at the party?

I'm not angry. I'm worried that you are trying too hard for the people around you.

Do you mean Mom? Because Mom's whole life is about connecting. She brings people together. It's her way of being generous. She doesn't care if I'm weird as long as I can connect. Does this make sense to you, Layla?

Instead of answering, Layla sent me a link to one of her articles about the neurodiversity movement. I already knew about this movement that wants society to accept people on the autistic spectrum for who they are instead of trying to cure them. But I'd never read an argument this clear. I couldn't believe it. It was like I'd been color-blind my whole life and now suddenly I wasn't. Everything looked different.

I read the article five times. In one section, it compared being on the autistic spectrum to being gay. Here is what it argued: Autism is not a problem to be fixed. It's a way to be. Homosexuality is no longer called a disease. So why is autism?

The article quoted an autism rights activist named Jim Sinclair. He wrote:

> It is not possible to separate the autism from the person . . . Therefore, when parents say, "I wish my child did not have autism," what they're

really saying is, "I wish the autistic child I have did not exist and I had a different (non-autistic) child instead." Read that again. This is what we hear when you mourn over our existence. This is what we hear when you pray for a cure. This is what we know, when you tell us of your fondest hopes and dreams for us: that your greatest wish is that one day we will cease to be, and strangers you can love will move in behind our faces.

Did everyone around me dream of turning me into a stranger?

My fingers trembled as I texted Layla. **Thank you for the article. I am very glad you exist.**

She texted back a video of her hands on the piano. They were playing "Let It Be."

## 11:25 p.m.

Tonight was balmy. Mom, Elisabeth, Arthur, Asparagus Man, and I ate leftovers from the party out on the terrace. I had two pieces of clafoutis. Arthur said he was glad that Bernadette had not caved by pitting the cherries. This made me like him a lot. He is becoming less of a fur ball and more of a person. He's skinny, not very tall, and he has a high forehead like Elisabeth's, but no widow's peak. Mom has stopped making comments about the age difference between Arthur and Elisabeth. She says Arthur is winning her over.

During dessert, Asparagus Man went inside to do the dishes. He was facing out the kitchen window above the sink, which was open onto the terrace. We could hear the water running. He didn't want clafoutis because he says that Mom is making him fat. He says this a lot. He laughs loudly every time he says it.

The cottage has a dishwasher, but it is very tiny, and Mom says it's not worth it. She says using a dishwasher in the French countryside feels vulgar when everything here is on such a human scale. Asparagus Man appears to agree with her. When he is at work at the sink, he whistles.

What bothers me about him most is that he's inserted himself inside our world as if there's always been a place for him here and we've been waiting for him to fill it. He acts way too comfortable. How can anyone step into a family and instantly behave as though they fit, with no familiarity, no repetition, no practice? It makes no sense to me. Intimacy is not like that. Even for people they call neurotypical. Asparagus Man must be a fake.

He was rinsing and clinking. Mom, Elisabeth, and Arthur were drinking wine.

I was trying to decide if I should say something about Layla's article. Then I did.

"Mom, what if I was gay?"

"You're not gay!" Mom said more loudly than she needed to, since there was no other talking to drown out. Then she did some of her yoga breaths, which helped her speak more softly. "Of course, it's fine if you are gay. It never occurred to me. But I would be fine with it. Just fine. Are you gay, Martin?"

"No. I'm making an analogy."

"Between what and what?" Mom asked. "I'm a little confused."

"I'm finding out that there are a lot of us who hate that the world is trying to cure us. I think the point is that we don't need to be cured, like gay people don't need to be cured. A lot of us believe that."

"A lot of *us*? A lot of who, Martin?"

"Autistic people who say that autism is a way to be in the world, like being gay. Not a disability. Not a disease. Some of us are offended at the idea that we need to be cured. Layla says it attacks us at our core."

"So, you believe you're always going to be autistic?" Mom's face pinched. Her eyes got watery. "But we were trying . . ." She trailed off. I could tell she didn't want to say anything too fast because it was complicated and she didn't want to hurt my feelings. "Anything that is a part of your identity is fantastic, Martin. We all want you to be happy. You need the tools. That's all. We don't want to force anything on you. We want you to be able to be happy. We want to give you the tools."

When she gets nervous, Mom repeats herself.

"Papa says that happiness is overrated."

"Does he?" She reared her head like a startled snake. "It's fair to say that, at this point, your father is not in a position to make such grand pronouncements, is he?"

"Do you hate Papa?"

"No, but I'm very disappointed in him."

"He used to say you are disappointed a lot because of your high standards. He said they weren't realistic."

"He might have been right. But my personal standards aren't the only issue here."

"So, do you still want to cure me?"

"Martin, I want what you want. What's this really about? Is it school, or your new friends? You've been doing so well."

"Do you think that what I am is 'sick'? Do you think I'm mentally ill and I need to be changed?"

"No. I don't. I don't know."

Mom suddenly looked at Arthur, who was holding Elisabeth's hand. He was staring up into the sky. I do this too, when I don't want the people around to worry about me. It's a way to be absent when you're there.

"Might I add," Asparagus Man called out from the open kitchen window, "that there was a French philosopher who said that mental illness is only real within a culture that recognizes it as such?"

"Foucault said that," said Elisabeth. She's so smart. I don't know who Foucault is, but she was obviously right because Asparagus Man clucked and Mom nodded. I asked Elisabeth how to spell the name, and she told me. She was massaging the air with her spidery fingers. She turned to Asparagus Man, who was walking out of the kitchen, drying his hands on a blue dish towel. She asked: "So you're saying that mental illness is in the eye of the beholder?"

"He's not mentally ill!" Mom yelled. She started her deep breathing again. She tried to drink wine at the same time that she was inhaling, and she choked.

I patted her back. Her spine is like a rope.

"Martin." Elisabeth sounded angry. "It's easy for you to spout stuff about neurodiversity when you are high-functioning and could almost pass for nothing more than quirky. Do you honestly believe the really autistic

185

people, the ones in diapers who bang their heads against walls, would advocate for themselves to stay that way? I would guess not. I'd like to help them become capable of making up their own minds."

"Layla hates it when people say 'quirky,'" I said. "She says that 'quirky' is an offensive euphemism." I mostly said this to give myself time to think about what Elisabeth meant.

"What does Layla have to do with anything?" Elisabeth snapped. Then she looked at Arthur, who was still staring at the sky but was now rubbing her shoulders. Right away, she said, "I'm sorry, Martin."

I tried not to look away but my gaze flew up to the stars. I began to count them so I wouldn't start to rock or groan.

"Sweetheart," Mom said to Elisabeth, "Layla is Martin's closest friend. Of course he should be able to bring her into any discussion."

"No one has answered my question about curing me," I reminded them.

Then Mom said, "Martin, if someday you end up complaining to your shrink—or your girlfriend, or your wife—that I made you do too much therapy, then I will be satisfied that I've done my job."

"I'm sorry, Martin," Elisabeth said again. She stood up

and walked over to me. She took my chin gently and pulled it downward so that our eyes met.

"Whoa!" Asparagus Man laughed much too loudly. And then he made his point again, even though we were all way beyond it now. "I don't mean to start a fight here. I'm only saying there is a school of thought that would say people, like for example Martin, are only divergent if that's how they are labeled. If there's no label, there's no reality."

"I don't get it," I said. I stopped counting stars. I had gotten to thirty-four. I looked down at my sneakers.

Of course, I understood what Asparagus Man meant, but I didn't want to engage with him. I wanted him to realize that he was being inappropriate. I wanted him to shut up. And so I pretended to be confused to make him uncomfortable. This is what they call "disingenuous." It's new for me.

"It's late, everyone," Mom said. She stood up and stretched. Elisabeth, Arthur, and Asparagus Man all stood up and stretched too. I was the only one who did not move.

They all said it was time for bed. I said I was going to stay outside for a while and count more stars. Nobody tried to change my mind.

They all went inside, except Arthur, who gave Elisabeth

a kiss and told her he would see her tomorrow. He smiled at me, picked up his bag from the ground, then looked up at the sky, like he was going to count stars too. My chest tightened. I wanted him to leave. I wanted to be alone.

Here is a list of the things I was feeling: pride, appreciation, sadness, gratitude, worry, anger, fear, loneliness, hope.

"Martin, I just wanted to say, the questions you are asking are interesting."

His voice was not too loud and did not clash with the cricket song.

"Thank you," I said, still looking up. I started to relax.

"I feel strange sometimes too," he said. "Like I see stuff backward."

"What do you mean?" I asked.

"When I'm working, I'm not looking at the movie while it's being shot. The whole time I'm planning and I'm thinking about what it will look like to people when it's done. But I'm not there."

"That's cool," I said. "But it could make it hard to appreciate life while it's happening."

"Yep."

I turned from the stars to his face. "Does my sister tell you to live in the moment?"

He laughed through his beard. "Yeah, she does."

"I always try to listen to my sister."

"That's probably a good policy." The crickets got suddenly louder, but he did not raise his voice to compete with them. I liked this. "Do you want to be by yourself?" he asked. "I'll get going."

"I don't mind if you stay." I meant it.

"Thanks," he said.

We counted stars for a while. When I got to fifty-one, which was Proust's age when he died, I asked, "Do you think my questions have answers?"

He laughed again softly. "Oh, yes, all kinds of answers."

We didn't talk again for a while, but I stopped counting stars and tried to make a list of different possible answers. Only I was too tired.

Arthur said it was good hanging out and goodnight.

I said goodnight too. I watched his back as he walked to his car. I watched his headlights go on. They reminded me of a pair of big, kind eyes.

# Monday, June 13
## 5:45 p.m.

I imagined that since I invited the moths to the party and tried hard to include them, that we were all finally friends. I was wrong. I'm an idiot.

Every time Mr. Swann starts to believe Odette is faithful, she does something cruel. Like she tells him he can't come with her to Madame Verdurin's salon. Or she makes fun of him in public. Or she lies about where she's been and who she's been with. And whenever Marcel starts to hope that Gilberte is happy to see him in the Champs-Élysées, she lets him know there's somewhere else she'd rather be.

At lunch today, Marianne said thanks for inviting her with the group to the party. She said she really couldn't believe I wasn't on Facebook or Instagram. She got all animated, like a Center kid with an obsession. Marianne is still not totally clear to me, but there are some things I'm sure of: her purple hair streaks, her pale skin, and her low voice that booms sometimes. She kept booming, "Really? It's not possible that you don't want to try it! Really? You're joking?!"

I told her I really didn't want to. It would be over-whelming. Toxic.

People say I'm wrong. Social media would be helpful to me because of the emotional distance. I don't buy it. My mind is noisy enough.

Marianne wouldn't listen. She shoved her phone in front of me, saying, "Let me show you how it works! I'll set you up an account. You'll love it."

I said technology isn't my issue. I know how to set up accounts if I want them. She paid zero attention. She was in the grips of an idea and couldn't control herself. She scrolled down on her phone to show me posts from her different friends. "See, you could talk to everyone and you wouldn't have to worry about being shy." She was acting like she was the first person ever to think of In-stagram as a plan for me.

I didn't want to be rude, but I also did not want to deal with her feed, which was making me nauseated.

I thought I was saved when the Giotto boys and Simon came up to our table to sit down with their trays. Then Marianne pushed her phone into my face to show me a picture of Simon and me at our party that Simon had posted. You could see Gloria Seegar in the background. "Look how cool!" she exclaimed. In the picture, Simon had his arm around my shoulders. I was smiling stiffly. I looked less comfortable than I'd imagined at the time.

Suddenly, Marianne snatched the phone away, but not before I could read what Simon had written underneath the picture. *Le robot et moi.* The robot and me.

The truth slugged me.

I'm a robot. Even if I have volcanoes of emotion inside, I seem to these kids like some jerky robot. And Simon thinks it's funny. Alice probably does too.

They don't even care enough to unlock me. They don't think there's anything to unlock.

When I got up, Marianne followed me through the cafeteria. "I'm sorry, Martin! Don't be upset. Don't worry about Simon," she boomed. "He's being a clown. He doesn't mean it."

"Excuse me." I pushed past her without looking. I

rushed outside into the yard. You aren't supposed to go outside in the middle of lunch, but they don't make me follow the rules here. I might panic and malfunction.

This dream I've started having of passing in a non-special school, it's just that: a dream. Because even at the party, when I felt like I was doing great, I was still a total freak. Nothing has changed except that I have started to care.

I left school and walked all the way to the hawthorn bushes. I did not text Elisabeth because I did not want to have to explain anything.

I've put my sonata on loud. My book is open. I'm appreciating the flowers the way Mr. Swann appreciates a beautiful painting, after he's looked away for a while at something way less beautiful. I've been distracted by the French moths and the whole scene here, but now I'm back home. Home is *Search* and my headphones.

I focus on the flowers. I shape my fingers into a frame, so that I can't see anything else. I try to count blossoms. I keep losing count and having to start over.

I want to climb back inside the person I was before this all began.

I get a text from Alice, who is definitely not Gilberte anymore. She never was. She said: **Marianne told me about the misunderstanding. Can you talk?**

The misunderstanding? There is nothing to misunderstand. It's all perfectly clear. These kids have decided I don't feel anything. End of story. And if they knew me at all, they would stop trying to fool me with their sloppy language.

I don't answer her.

# Tuesday, June 14
## 12:20 p.m.

I refuse to go to school. School is a failed experiment. I've been moping around, staring into bowls of milky tea, memorizing the cracks in the ancient beams on our cottage ceiling, taking on cooking projects that involve a lot of repetitive prep. I've been chopping onions, peeling toasted hazelnuts, and plucking oregano leaves. I made trout with almonds last night from Julia Child. I was the only one who ate it. And I've made four quatre-quarts cakes from Papa's and my recipe that are a thousand times better than in the cafeteria at school. Why did I ever like that stupid industrial cake?

No one eats what I cook. Mom is behind schedule at

Chenonceau and is working until late at night. She is too busy to focus on me staying home. She says that as long as my Center work is getting handed in, she can't force me to do anything. I emailed the last of my assignments for the school year yesterday, a take-home test in pre-calculus and a short paper on *The Catcher in the Rye* that I titled "Phonies Rule."

Asparagus Man hasn't been here the past three nights. Elisabeth has pretty much stopped eating.

This morning, Mom told Elisabeth that starving herself was an "unimaginative response" to being in a fight with Arthur. Mom was drinking her coffee fast because she was late to shoot a crowd scene. She kept puckering her lips because the coffee, which she takes black, was burning her mouth. She was running her hands quickly through her hair. Papa used to say he loved her hair and that she should never color it. So far she hasn't, which gives me hope.

Elisabeth got mad at Mom. "So, you think I can control my response? Like I can just pick up my psych text-book and choose a more worthwhile way to feel? Not all of us are as perfect as you are, Mom. I'm not like you, okay. I'm sorry if I don't live up to your standards."

I could see Elisabeth's point that the ways we react to sad events are not always logical. But I also hear her calling Jason's new actress girlfriend a skinny bitch. This helps me understand why Mom would worry about her not eating my cooking.

Mom did not reply to Elisabeth. Instead she asked me if I was sure I didn't want to go with her today to see my friend Simon in the big funeral scene she'd cast him in. Even though her voice was gentle, her forehead was very creased, which meant she was anxious.

I didn't say that Simon was not my friend. I said that I did not feel like going, which was true.

The idea of seeing "Gilberte's" parents working in the gardens of the château made me sick. In my head, I listed the flowers I used to picture them planting: petunias, tobacco, Lilliput dahlias, impatiens, verveine, begonias. I listed the trees in the Green Garden: three planes, three blue cedars, two magnolias, one Spanish fir, one catalpa, one chestnut, two Douglas firs, two sequoias, one two-hundred-year-old holm oak tree, one white acacia, one black walnut.

These lists felt old and stale.

There is no mythical place called Chenonceau, inhabited by the mythical parents of a mythical girl. I don't need to go deal with a crowd of extras in stupid costumes to understand how wrong I've been. It's already clear.

"I really, really don't want to go, Mom. Sorry."

197

Mom sighed. "Are you sure, Martin?" she asked. "You don't want to go to the shoot to see your friend?"

"Leave him alone," Elisabeth said.

I saw Mom's face crumple for a second, then reform itself. I suppose other faces do this. But I don't focus on many other faces. Hers is the only one I've ever seen leave and come back so instantly. She was worried about me. She would be relieved if I went with her to the set today and greeted Simon in his period costume. She would see things coming together. Like my normal friendship, and my normal friend being in her movie, and me acting normal in a big scene full of people. It would be the kind of "united" moment that Layla describes from *Downton Abbey.* For example, a wedding, or a Christmas party, or a village fair, where you get the Grantham family and the servants all interacting together. If I'd gone today, Mom would have been so incredibly happy. But I couldn't do it. Not even for her.

I'm having what Proust calls an "involuntary memory." It's a memory of a conversation. The conversation happened when I was fifteen, two months before Papa left. Three things reminded me of it.

1. Elisabeth turning a page in her biology textbook sounded like Papa turning a page of his

book about the history of World War II in our living room.

2. Bernadette's teakettle whistled like Mom's teakettle back in our kitchen.
3. A napkin on my cheek reminded me of the sheets
   where I buried my face while Mom and Papa were
   arguing.

I heard Papa turn a page, then slam his book onto the
coffee table. "Sam, did you know that before Hitler
started euthanizing Jews he started out by euthanizing
disabled children?" Papa's voice caught. "Tens of thousands of disabled children."

"Martin is not disabled. He's not a cripple, okay? Stop
worrying retrospectively. Or hypothetically. Or whatever." Her voice was angry.

Papa kept talking like he hadn't heard her. "Before
Martin was born, I never would have imagined wanting
a disabled child. Now I love him so much that I love autism. That's why this killing them is so, so horrible. How
can life be about anything besides wanting your child to
thrive? Martin has reshaped me, Sam."

"Shut up, okay?" Mom screamed. Her teakettle whistled. It stopped.

"What's so wrong?" His tone got even sadder.

"Paul," she hissed, "it's pretty galling to hear you talk about ethics. To drag our son into your story like some kind of cover for what you did. It's not like we needed the money for his therapy bills. You happen to be married to one of the most successful women in Hollywood. But that's the story you're telling yourself. That it was all justified because you were trying to save Martin from whatever you imagine he needs saving from. It's sick. Doesn't the disconnect strike you?"

I was lying in bed repeating everything they said under my breath. By the age of fifteen, I had enough self-control not to be loud enough for them to overhear. And I was smart enough to understand that Papa's crime was my fault. He *was* trying to save me. Trying to save me made him lose sight of reality.

In the pause after Mom's words, I had time to repeat her question—"Doesn't the disconnect strike you?"—three times, in a whisper, before Papa spoke back.

When he finally spoke, he said, "You can't compare me to the Nazis, Sam. I haven't murdered anyone."

"How do you know?" She was screaming again. "People do kill themselves over this kind of thing. And lives are ruined. You don't even realize what you've done. You don't see all the repercussions. How could you?"

This is where I stopped listening. I hid my face in my sheets and repeated the question, "How could you? How could you? How could you?" until the words lost meaning.

# Wednesday, June 15
## 2:10 p.m.

Alice texted me again this morning. She texted an emoji of a madeleine next to the number sixteen followed by a question mark. She's asking me to meet her at sixteen hours, or 4:00 p.m., for madeleines.

She's an imposter and I should ignore her. She's not a friend. The thing is, though, that I'm dying to go meet her. I want to send her back a heart emoji with an arrow through it. My body aches for her. My knee wants her hand on it again. I want to kiss her.

In my postcard collection is a painting called *Lost*

*Illusions*, by a nineteenth-century painter named Charles Gleyre. It's a Romantic painting of a party of people who look Roman to me. They're getting onto a Viking boat under a crescent moon. Marcel wrote that the moon in Gleyre's landscapes was cut out against the sky like a silver sickle. Papa chose this postcard for me. He wrote a note on the back, covering both the message area and the part where the address should go. He put it for me on the kitchen counter the day he left for five years in prison. I'm holding it right now in my left hand. My feet are in our pool.

Here is what Papa wrote:

*Dear Martin,*

*I am very sorry for what I have done, and especially sorry that I have to leave you. I feel nothing but admiration for you. The ability to communicate that most of us acquire instinctively, stupidly almost, like animals, is something that you have acquired through discipline, reading, and deep thought. With one book, you've taught yourself to see how another person perceives. You've found empathy. I have every confidence in you and in the fruits of YOUR Search. Remember, it's not what's inside the madeleine. It's what's inside you. I love you.*

*Papa*

While I was reading Papa's card, Elisabeth came to the pool with a glass of lemonade for me. She sat down next to me, handed me the lemonade, and began to dangle her toes next to mine in the cold water.

Today, Elisabeth is wearing the dress with the hawthorn flowers. She is barefoot. Her hair is swept into a bun. She has shadows under her eyes, but she is smiling.

"Why are you looking at me like you're trying to remember something?" she asked. She used her gently teasing voice. I wondered if her fight with Arthur was over.

"I'm trying to figure out if you look like someone from one of my postcards right now."

"How about the Botticelli? She's hot. I'll take her. And no way am I that Giotto *Charity* one. She's gnarly."

I recognized this as a joke, and I laughed.

My mind was still on Alice's text. I was having all kinds of bright images of meeting her for madeleines, but I couldn't decide if I should.

My confusion must have shown on my face, because

the next thing my sister said was, "Why the frown? Are you worried about something?"

I asked her if she remembered Alice from the big dinner. She said of course she did. Then I told her that Alice, Simon, and the other kids from school are all moths drawn to the flame of glamour like the ones Layla draws on my Converses whenever I get a new pair. I told her about how at first Alice was Gilberte from *Search*. When the differences appeared, and I realized she was Alice, I still liked her. I told her about Alice's letter admitting that she and the others had only been friendly to get close to Mom's movie and the actors. I described my reaction in the bathroom, which proved to me that original speech is basically an illusion. Then I told her about my translating at the party, about the amazing feeling of unlocking a world for other people. Then I told her about Marianne's Instagram feed and being called a robot. Robots have no emotions. They're not general-ed, but they are not neurodiverse either.

"Robots," I said, "are neuronothing."

Elisabeth was staring hard into the place where the sun hit the pool. She stares this way when she imagines being a therapist. "You didn't mind so much if your friends were betraying you as long as they made it clear that they were betraying a human being. That's why Alice's letter wasn't a deal breaker, right?"

I nodded.

Elisabeth said she thought the robot comment seemed especially cruel because it suggested that Simon didn't consider me human. She asked if she was right.

I told her she was right about Simon, but that I can handle cruelty. I have fantastic literary models for cruelty and suffering. I can take abuse. What I can't take is not existing.

"Martin," she said, "you are missing out on some subtleties here."

Missing out on subtleties is one of my specialties.

"I wonder if this robot thing is as big a deal as you perceive." She hesitated. "Can I take a stab at some perspective?"

She took my hand.

"Kids coin nicknames sometimes that work as a kind of shorthand. The names themselves don't necessarily carry that much weight. Your friends might even have meant *le robot* affectionately, half as a joke, because sometimes, Martin, you can come off as quite formal with your precise vocabulary. It's about your mannerisms, not about you. It's meant to be funny, not true. And let's take the worst-case scenario, that it's an insult, okay? So it's Simon's insult, not Alice's. Alice is the one who wrote you the letter, remember? *She's* cool."

"So I'm getting it wrong?"

"You say that like it's a crime. Getting it wrong is the most human thing there is." She looked at her pale feet in the water and pointed her toes, which have lavender polish on the nails. "I was up with Arthur most of last night because we were figuring out something we both misunderstood. He thought that I still wanted to be with Jason because I made some jealous comment about Jason's skinny new actress girlfriend. I guess I'm a little fixated on her, but that doesn't mean I like Jason anymore, or that I want him back. I can't stand Jason. Arthur is so much more wonderful. I was treating Arthur like I could tell him every negative idea that passes through me, I guess because I trust him. Only I have to understand that it's not all about me. And it's not all about him either. Does that make any sense?"

"Yes," I said, but not because it made sense. I said it because I wanted this moment to be about her and not me. "Did you work it out?" I asked. I was asking because I cared. Because I like Arthur.

"Yeah, we're going to be great."

"That's awesome," I said.

She squeezed my hand. "Now what are we going to do about Alice?" she asked.

"She's asked me to meet her today. At the bakery, for madeleines. We've already been once together and we had a good time, or at least I did. Should I go again?"

"Of course you should. Are you sure she's aware of the robot thing?"

"Everyone's aware of everything." This was an exaggeration. I don't usually exaggerate. It felt weird, like I was suddenly doing the splits when I never could before.

"You should go see her if she's asking. Give her a chance."

When Elisabeth said this, it was 2:00 p.m. I asked her if she would drive me to town at 3:30 p.m.

She said yes.

### 3:45 p.m.

Marcel first hears the name "Gilberte!" flying across the park, through a crowd of children and their nannies. It's like magic after so many years of dreaming about her. The name goes whizzing like a ball in the air, aiming for a target.

208

Hearing Gilberte's name is awesome, but it's also a reminder that Marcel is not the one calling her. It's the caller who actually knows her. Not Marcel. The caller gets to fling Gilberte's name with "a lighthearted cry." Marcel just gets to listen. Even though he's getting closer, Marcel is an outsider. Like me, waiting in the small green square outside the *boulangerie* for Alice, a boy trapped inside a robot.

# Thursday, June 16
## 10:30 p.m.

She kisses you. No kidding. For real. On the bench, on the lips. She says, "Robots can't kiss. So you can't be a robot." Then she laughs.

Kissing is uncomfortable, but it is the kind of uncomfortable that you crave at the same time that it makes you anxious. It's like being tickled. You can't stand it, but as soon as it stops you want it again. Really badly.

She says she didn't realize how much she liked you until she thought you were mad at her and wouldn't see her anymore. When you miss a person is when you know they are important.

Alice explains about Simon. "He couldn't understand

why you weren't more mad when you found out about how the group was using you for the party and the movie scenes. He said that you didn't ever get pissed off. You were bizarrely cool. Robotic. Simon gets angry a lot. He hits people and breaks stuff. So you being so cool about us using you, this didn't make sense to him. Like you can't be a real boy if you don't get mad. The rest of us, we convinced him he was being stupid. Then we made a joke that you are a sweet robot, like R2-D2 in Star Wars, the cute little guy. So it was funny. Especially since you are so tall." She stops and looks straight at you. "Don't worry so much about it," she says.

You say you aren't worried anymore and that it is time to buy madeleines.

She laughs again. "What a great idea," she says.

You go into the bakery and buy a bag of madeleines. Outside the bakery, she takes your hand and starts to lead you out of the square. She wants to walk to Chenonceau to watch the funeral scene for Henri II. It's in its second day of shooting. You will see Simon, Michel, Georges, and Kevin. Mom has cast them all.

Walking takes half an hour. Alice holds your hand the whole time. She bites her nails. Her green nail polish is almost all worn away.

The castle, clouds, and trees are perfectly reflected

in the river. It is a painting. Until you and Alice get close and go into the gardens, and the place comes alive.

Lots of people at Chenonceau are in Renaissance costume for Mom's movie. Your friends from school are wearing tights, bloomer shorts, and blouses. Mom has them lined up with the other extras along the main *allée* of the château. Asparagus Man is standing next to Mom, watching the action on a screen. When he winks at you, you don't even mind.

You say hi to Arthur, who looks preoccupied.

You do something you've never done before. You imagine watching this scene from Mom's movie, on a day in the future, with Layla in her basement, while thinking back to these moments at Chenonceau. Does this mean you are getting what they call "sequencing"? Does this looking ahead make you a more normal kid? Or does it show you that you are unique, because no one else in the world but you will watch Mom's movie with Layla in her basement while recalling Asparagus Man's wink and recognizing the cool kids from school dressed up in tights, pretending to be all depressed because King Henri is dead, when they are really completely happy to be in Mom's movie?

During a break, Simon comes over to you and Alice. His shoes are dusty brown leather slippers instead of Doc

Martens. You manage to look up into his face, where you see two competing things. He is looking at you. At the same time he is constantly glancing at Gloria Seegar, who is talking to Mom. Gloria is wearing a black silk dress. There are strings of black beads all through her hair.

"*Ça va?*" he asks. You are surprised to hear in his "*Ça va?*" the question, "Are you angry?"

You catch your breath. How could Simon be playing Papa's *Ça va* game if he isn't a true friend?

"*Ça va,*" you answer, meaning, "I don't think I'm angry anymore." "*Et toi, ça va?*" meaning, "And you, are you feeling sorry?"

"*Ça va,*" he replies, meaning, "Yes, I'm sorry."

By the time you get to the end of the *Ça va*s, you and Simon are okay.

You meet Alice's mother. She is nothing like Odette. She does not wear a purple wrap of crepe de Chine or a pink silk dress with a strand of pearls. She wears green cargo pants and work boots, and she does not act like a snob. Her face is tanned and wrinkled from working in the sun. She has freckles. She does not force eye contact.

Alice says to you, "Let's go to Catherine de Médicis's private garden to see the roses and orange trees." You wander together away from the crowd. On a hill of lavender sloping down to the castle's moat, she says she wants to listen to your music. You share earbuds and lie down on the ground staring at the sky, holding hands.

When the sonata is over, she rolls to face you and asks, "Can I ask you a question?"

You nod. You are interested in what her question is going to be, but you are more interested in kissing her again.

She speaks softly because she is very close to you. "I know you don't like being called a robot, but do you like being different? Or do you even feel different from other people?"

"You want to kiss," is all you can say. It comes out as a flat statement, rather than a question.

She does not seem to mind how inappropriate your response is. "Okay," is all she says, and then she waits with her mouth hanging in the air a breath away from yours. She waits for you to cross the space, which you do. You pull her into you.

Everywhere her body meets yours, a little wall tumbles down.

"I really like you," Alice whispers in between two kisses.

Alice calls me "you." So "you" has been right all along.

# Friday, June 17
## 4:30 p.m.

I've gone back to school.

And I'm going to go to Simon's party tomorrow. I will recognize enough people there for it to be okay. Besides, Alice will help me. She talks a lot about how Simon misses his dad. It's why he sometimes drinks too much. The thing we have to watch, she says, is that Simon doesn't get so wasted that he gets totally sick all over his house while his mom is away.

I haven't said anything more to Layla about the moth party. She doesn't know I've decided to go for sure. Ever since she started sending me stuff about the neurodiversity movement, I'm avoiding mentioning my general-ed friends. I'm scared that if I tell her that I am going to Simon's house to drink beer on a Saturday night, she'll say that I am "living vicariously" through these neurotypical kids.

I could argue back that she and I are vicarious people. But I won't.

Instead of telling her about my real teenage plans for the weekend, I tell her about cooking rabbit with prunes. It was the first thing Elisabeth ate after she made up with Arthur. I also give Layla descriptions of my buzzing-fly music, the rhubarb jam on baguettes in the morning, and the hawthorns I still visit every day. I want her to believe that I am still me.

She is smarter than that.

**How are the French moths? How is it that you are not mentioning them these days? How is Gilberte? Do you think our phones are instruments of communication or torture?**

Layla has latched on to The Center's questioning strategy. She's become such a master of the question that she can parody it. She's playing with me because I'm not telling her everything.

I answer her text: **Moths got to be extras in a big scene in the movie. Funeral for the king, killed jousting. The dead king used to be Peter Bird. Gloria is** queen. Fuchsia is mistress. Moths delighted. Only Gilberte wasn't in it. And her name is really Alice.

How is she? Will you be going to Simon's general-ed party?

After behavioral therapy, it's almost impossible for me not to answer a direct question. But I figure something out. Instead of responding to her questions, I ask her my own. This is another way to show empathy and interest.

What is your favorite episode of Season Three? Who is your favorite Beatle?

Episode seven, when Bates is freed from prison. Paul. I am still waiting to find out how Gilberte is. How are your plans for the general-ed party faring or not faring?

*"Merde,"* as Papa would say.

I just told you Gilberte's real name is Alice. She isn't from the book. But it's okay. I will go to the party with no illusions. Don't worry.

Then she texts a video of her big, beautiful hands playing the chorus to "Yesterday" while she sings along. "Oh, I believe in yesterday."

The sound of her voice brings me back to the music room at The Center. Thanks to movie-industry donors with special-needs kids like us, the music room at The Center is state of the art. Most important for Layla, it has a Steinway baby grand. Her voice bounces off the padded walls as she plays and sings. She says "Yesterday" is my song because I'm so into nostalgia, being a Proustian and all. She loves to sing me this song. It's her idea of a joke that never gets unfunny.

Only, I'm starting to think that Layla is the nostalgic one. She's the one who doesn't want us to change.

# Saturday, June 18
## 3:20 p.m.

I haven't taken my headphones off all day. I can barely look at anyone, not Mom, not Elisabeth, not Arthur, and especially not Asparagus Man.

Everyone is hanging around the house because there is some big official event at Chenonceau, so there can be no shooting. To fill the day, Baxter Wolff organized a private tour of another château, called Chambord, but none of us wanted to go. We are all exhausted. This morning, we slept until eleven. Breakfast tasted like metal. Even the rhubarb jam.

I can't go to Simon's party. I'm so nervous about it that I've spent hours pacing around the cottage, staring at my shoes. The outlines of Layla's silver moths are burned into my eyes.

I'm not scared of being laughed at. I'm scared of drowning. I'm scared I'll forget my basic skills: pass the ball back and forth; pass the words back and forth. I'll drop everything. Alice will abandon me. It will all become chaos.

Only if I stay away, the moths will figure I haven't understood that the robot thing was only a joke. It'll make them feel unforgiven. Alice will think her kisses didn't mean enough, which is not true. And I'll also disappoint everyone here at home. Elisabeth has said she will drive me to the party and pick me up at any time. I don't want to see her face struggle to stop looking sad if I don't go. Arthur has said that if he were my age, I would be the kid he would want to hang out with. I don't want him to think I'm ignoring him. I don't want Mom to ask, "Are you sure?" And I really don't want Asparagus Man to quote Foucault at me.

But I don't want to go to the damn party. I should stay home tonight. I should stay inside my head, and be proud of who I am.

# Sunday, June 19
## 3:10 a.m.

I did go to Simon's. Here is what happened:

When Elisabeth asked me what time I wanted to leave the cottage, I told her I wasn't sure I could do it. I was all geared up for her bad reaction. Only there was no reaction. She didn't try to convince me to go. She only said to tell her if I changed my mind. Her voice was flat, but I didn't detect irritation. She went back to having Arthur quiz her on chemical compounds with multicolored flash cards.

Then Mom mentioned that a group of people were planning to meet some of the cast for dinner at Baxter's place. He'd hired a famous chef and challenged him to make a paleo meal. Paleo means eating the way they figure prehistoric people ate, with fish, meat, and vegetables, and almost no grains, dairy, or starches. It's fashionable. Mom thinks it's funny. She said she's sure that, even if the chef has to work within the rules of the paleo diet, the result will be spectacular, "kind of like Shakespeare working within the confines of the sonnet." If I didn't feel like going to Simon's party, she said I should come with her and Joe, aka Asparagus Man, to Baxter's instead because it would be an experience.

Asparagus Man seconded her invitation to the paleo dinner.

I got a text from Alice saying that she would understand if the party didn't sound fun to me and that we could hang out soon.

There was no pressure on me to go. And suddenly I wanted to go. I had a burst of confidence. Alice would be happy to see me. And so would everyone else.

Simon lives in a housing development on a street called rue Racine. His house is white and cracked with a rusty swing set in the yard for his little brother.

When Elisabeth pulled in front of the house, there were eight mopeds parked along the low concrete wall by the street. In the yard, we saw a green plastic table with sodas, beers, and a big bowl of chips on it, along with a few smaller bowls of what they call *gâteaux apéritifs*, which are the salty snacks they have here with drinks, little pretzels, and tiny orange crackers. Mom says *gâteaux apéritifs* are tacky, not to mention gross. For before dinner, she prefers pistachios and crudités. I'm sure Marcel's grandmother would agree. But neither of them would ever come to a party at Simon's.

"This is your first *boum*," said Elisabeth when the Smart car stopped.

*Boum* is slang for a party.

"Yeah," I said.

"Okay, so this isn't a teaching moment. It's more of a going-for-it moment. Just one thing: try not to drink too much. Your body isn't used to it."

"Okay."

"Have fun. Text me when you want to come home. I'm not going to the paleo dinner. I have to work. Arthur says he'll keep me company but I told him he should go if he wants."

The Smart car drove off. Elisabeth was disappearing along with it. My mind can't hold her back anymore. She is going away from me, to Stanford and then to become a real doctor. My bubble is getting thinner.

There is a crowd of mostly familiar shoes on the hard brown grass of Simon's small yard, next to the green table with the snacks. Simon is handing me a beer, which foams when I pull the tab, spilling over. I watch the foam bubble on the grass by my foot.

Techno music starts to play on a weak sound system. It's a good thing the sound is not strong because, even though I like repetition, that single relentless beat makes me insane.

My first sip of beer spreads through me, putting some distance between the music and me. When I take another sip, the music gets even further away. My skin stops tingling from the stress of it. I get more comfortable. A few more sips and I stop caring about the stupid techno beat. I glance up from the ground to see faces. A Giotto boy smiles at me. Kevin.

Where is Alice?

Some time has passed. The sun is setting. It must be after 9:00 p.m. I have had three beers and three large handfuls of chips.

Simon is wasted. I have seen enough people at Mom's parties to recognize when a person is drunk. They touch you too freely and get too close to you when they talk. It can be scary. All that sloppy affection. Only with Simon, it's okay when he puts his skinny arm around my shoulders because it helps me keep my balance, since, for the first time, I'm drunk too.

He jokes that R2-D2 is not such a bad nickname.

"I understand," I say.

"No," Simon says, "you don't understand. Do you get exactly why I called you a robot?"

I say that I have a few ideas but that I am not sure which one is right. I say, let's talk about something else.

He does not talk about something else. He says he still can't believe that I didn't get furious when Alice wrote me that letter about the party. Like I'm a different species from him because I don't have anger. He's sorry he called me a robot, but that's what he meant. "You don't defend yourself," he says. "You're missing something," he says, "in your personality." Is he saying I have a screw loose? Because I don't get mad enough? Because I don't rage?

I have no idea how to respond to Simon.

Someone has found a way to make the music louder. It's starting to bug me again. I reach for a cube of cheese on a toothpick. It's full of holes, so it's probably Appenzeller.

Simon keeps talking. He says he is especially angry a lot of the time because of his dad. So maybe that's why he doesn't get how someone like me can forgive things. "You can't know what it's like to have a dad in jail."

"But I told you! *My* dad *is* in jail!" I exclaim. I want him to see that we have this in common.

He takes his arm away from my shoulders and gives me a look I recognize as hostile. "Yeah, that's right, *my* dad is in jail. Why do you keep trying to copy me? Are you trying to be funny, or what?"

"No, I'm not trying to be funny," I say, forcing myself to stay calm. "*My* dad is in jail too. I mean it."

Simon turns his back on me.

I'm stunned. I was trying to bond with another boy my age whose dad is also in jail. I was finding common ground. And for once my pronoun wasn't even wrong.

Simon goes stiff for a few seconds, then he turns around. "You're serious, aren't you?"

I nod.

"If you want me to believe you, you're going to have to tell me what he did to end up there."

"He was working in finance, and he got confused and stole some money. Not on purpose. What about your dad?"

"He wasn't confused at all. He was an asshole. Very much on purpose. He sold amphetamines from his truck and didn't give his family any of the money. He probably spent it on whores. He got addicted himself. It was a nightmare."

"I'm sorry," I say.

"Me too," he says.

Alice appears. She's wearing a white halter top with white jeans, big hoop earrings, and green liquid eyeliner. Her lips are glossy. She is, for sure, not Gilberte anymore.

She glances around, then gives me a quick kiss. The gloss stays on my mouth. She says she's glad I decided to come. She says, let's go to the kitchen to hang out. Since the techno music is coming from the kitchen, I ask if she minds if we stay outside. She says fine. We go to a corner of the hedge that separates Simon's house from his neighbors'.

Here Alice takes both my hands and kisses me. Her kisses have already become a habit, and it would hurt if they got taken away.

"Is Simon being okay to you? It looked like he was yelling there for a minute."

"No, we're okay." I start thinking of a way to explain about our two dads and the similarity of their being in prison and the difference in their crimes.

But she keeps talking, and what she says makes me forget what I am going to say.

"It's not you, Martin. Don't take it personally. He needs to get mad in general. He gets mad at all of us. That's why

227

I stopped going out with him. He was too angry all the time."

"You went out with him?"

"You didn't know?"

I shake my head.

"That's okay," she says. "It was for a few weeks and it didn't work out."

"I'm sorry," I say reflexively. This is not true. I am not sorry that Alice does not go out with Simon anymore. I wish she had never gone out with him at all. The wish is a throbbing in my temples. I pull Alice close to me, only the pull is harder than it should be.

"Don't worry," she says, not pulling away even though I am squeezing her. "It was ages ago, like last year."

Unlike Mr. Swann, I do not assume she is lying.

Kevin and Marianne come to us with plastic glasses of red wine from a box with a spigot. I let go of Alice. We follow them back out into the party.

There are a couple of kids not from school, but who aren't completely foreign. They must be from the pool. We all stand around. I don't talk. I can't get over the fact that Simon used to kiss Alice. Still, I am happy to be the one holding Alice's hand tonight, although I notice she is looking around the yard a lot, searching for someone. Mr. Swann would be paranoid, but I think I can handle it.

Marianne opens a pack of cigarettes, and everyone except me starts smoking. There are plumes of smoke rising into the night. Alice offers me a drag. I nod and take the burning cigarette between my fingers the way I see the others do. When I suck on the filter, I start to choke so hard that I throw up beer and wine, chips and cheese, right into the middle of the circle of kids. Because of the carbonation in the beer, it all comes up fast, like sea spray. It splatters on some of the kids' shoes. Everyone backs away, scraping off their feet in the trampled grass.

"It's okay," Alice says, letting go of my hand. "I'll go get you a towel."

I don't run away from the others because I am ashamed. That's not the reason. I run away because I need to be in a safer place, by myself. After the circle around my vomit breaks up, I do not wait for Alice with the towel. Instead, I disappear into a narrow, calm space between the other side of Simon's house and the hedge. The place where we were talking before. She will understand. She will know where to find me.

I can breathe here, under the eave of Simon's roof and

the branches of a plane tree spreading over from the yard next door. Eventually, I stop shaking and rocking. I pull out my phone and text Elisabeth.

Elisabeth texts back that she's leaving the cottage now and will be here in fifteen minutes.

I send her back an emoji of a speeding runner, which means "Hurry, please."

While I am waiting for her in the shadows, I see Alice leaving the party with another boy on the back of a motorcycle. They are talking and laughing. I cannot make out individual words. As they pull out into the rue Racine, she grabs him tightly around the waist and burrows her face in his neck.

Even though I have been conditioned from *Search* to expect betrayal, I'm surprised. Shouldn't I be in a different story by now, where Alice and I are falling in love instead of me imagining things?

Guess not.

Suddenly, I picture Layla alone in her basement with her old *Downton* episodes, feeling jealous of my new friends and specifically of Alice. I want to tell her that there is no point in being jealous, because probably none of it is true. Not the friends and not Alice either.

I groan softly. I scrape my knuckles against the rough hedge until they start to bleed.

## 11:30 p.m.

Today, at 1:05 p.m., I got a text from Simon saying **Alice had an accident last night. Meet us at the hospital.**

I screamed. I started to cry.

I ran to Elisabeth.

When I showed her the text, Elisabeth stopped her work, even though she was in the middle of an online exam. She held me and gave me Kleenex and drove me here, which took twenty minutes. We arrived at 1:40 p.m. Elisabeth said it was no big deal about her exam. She said she was worried about Alice and about me. She didn't ask questions because she sensed I couldn't answer.

There were two reasons I couldn't answer questions about Alice.

1. I could not say what exactly had happened to her, although I figured that the moped she'd left Simon's party on had crashed.
2. I don't understand what my relationship with her is.

I assumed that because she kissed me, gave me compliments, wrote me the honest letter about the party, and made sure we stayed okay after the robot fiasco, we were falling in love. I was starting to believe that the heartbreak from *Search* would not happen for me. Then it did. After mentioning that she once dated Simon, she left me at Simon's party with a boy who drove a moped. Even if I become the most general-ed kid on the planet, I will never drive a moped.

Elisabeth offered to come into the hospital to help me find Simon and the others, and I said yes because I doubted I could negotiate the desks and corridors full of strangers. If a staff member found me banging my head against a wall or rocking in a plastic chair, I would never make it to Alice.

While Elisabeth was parking the car, Simon texted me again, telling me to come to the fourth floor. He gave me Alice's room number: 4254. Elisabeth said that this meant that Alice wasn't being operated on and must be stable. I wasn't sure I understood her logic, but I did not ask her about it. All I cared about was getting to see Alice. My heart was racing and my palms were sweating. I started running through the parking lot. Instead of trying to slow me down, Elisabeth kept up, which I was grateful for.

The hospital is old and sad. It is built out of concrete.

We rushed through the sad corridors. I could feel Alice suffering. She was in a lot of pain, and I needed it to go away. Elisabeth asked directions. I ran on auto-pilot, the way some kids play video games.

It was 2:07 p.m. when we found Simon, Marianne, and the Giotto boys here in the fourth-floor waiting room. There was also a man holding a sleeping baby in a sling. He was wearing black Nike sneakers. He was Alice's father. Alice's mother was in the room with her. Only her parents have been allowed to see her.

When we first got here, the group told Elisabeth and me the story. People kept talking over one another and interrupting. I concentrated on the thread of what happened by translating into English for Elisabeth, even though she could understand.

Alice had looked for me at Simon's party, they said, but she figured I must have gotten embarrassed about the puking thing and decided to take off. So she left with her cousin Max to buy cigarettes. Max was blotto. He swerved off the road into a field. He was only scratched. Alice hit a rock and had a concussion, so she had to stay in a room with no light and no sound. Two of her ribs were broken. The doctors had been worried that her lung might be punctured, but the X-rays came back fine. They were almost positive there was no brain damage, but they wanted to be safe.

Elisabeth didn't need me to translate all this for her.

233

It was a way for me to deal with what I was hearing. It bought me time.

No matter how much roaring there is inside me, I can appear like a stone when I'm stressed. I touched my face for a clue about how I seemed to the others, but only noticed that my skin was rougher than before.

I asked, "Is Gilberte awake?"

"Who is Gilberte?" asked Marianne.

"She's Alice," said Simon, looking straight at me. "Gilberte is Martin's name for Alice. I guess she reminds him of a Gilberte he used to know."

This was very kind of him. When I looked straight into his bloodshot eyes, he smiled. Alice is going to be okay. Because if Alice was dying or in big danger, he wouldn't be able to smile.

Understanding this was a huge relief. I was so grateful to him that I smiled back.

Our exchange might look general-ed, but it wasn't. There is no such thing as general-ed.

Elisabeth asked me if I wanted to stay at the hospital, even though no one would be allowed in to see Alice today. I said I wanted to stay no matter what. She said to text her when I was ready for her to come back.

Simon, Marianne, Kevin, Michel, Georges, and I sat in the waiting room. They were mostly on their phones.

Marianne did three Snapchat stories about us waiting. We drank oily shots of coffee from a vending machine out of tiny brown plastic cups. I had two, with lots of sugar, which made my heart gallop. I didn't mind. A speeding heart was right for the situation.

At 3:10 p.m., the others went outside to smoke. When they came back, it was 3:42 p.m.

I started listening to my sonata over and over.

At 6:00 p.m., I took a break from listening to send Layla a text about what had happened.

At 6:25 p.m., I got this reply: **How is Gilberte doing? She is not going to die. This hospitalization does not have any of the elements of Matthew's accident or of Sybil's preeclampsia, which effectively killed off their characters. Gilberte will survive.**

Layla still calls Alice "Gilberte" on purpose. Layla hasn't moved on. I didn't comment on this. I said, **Thank you, Layla.**

At 6:40 p.m., she sent me a video of herself playing "Here Comes the Sun." I unplugged my headphones to show my friends, who said that it was very cool and that their grandparents loved that song.

At 7:20 p.m., Alice's mother came in to say that Alice was awake, but was not allowed to open her eyes or talk yet. Alice's mother was wearing a large pink T-shirt and soft gray shorts, which I guessed she'd been sleeping in when she was woken up with news of the crash. She introduced me to Alice's father, Bruno Corot. I decided not to focus on the major differences between him and Mr. Swann, because there were too many to count. The fact that Mr. Swann would never wear a baby in a sling was enough for me to let go. Madame Corot introduced me to Monsieur Corot as a "friend" of Alice's, an *intime*.

Both Alice's parents had deep shadows under their eyes and gray skin, but they did not look terrified.

Once, I saw the father of a girl from The Center rush to see her in the street after she was hit by a car. I did not see the girl get hit, but other kids did. They said her teeth flew out of her mouth. Her father was howling. His face was contorted. His face was the worst thing I have ever seen.

Monsieur and Madame Corot were not contorted, but they were exhausted and anxious. They looked like me: shaken but also grateful.

Madame Corot left with the baby, who had woken up. Then Monsieur Corot disappeared down the hallway toward Alice's room.

After so much time in the waiting room, I started getting used to it. There were two blue plastic sofas, six

blue plastic chairs, and two framed posters of Chenonceau. A row of windows looked out on the parking lot,
which was half full of small European cars.

At 8:56 p.m., while the dusk was falling outside, a
nurse came in and told us we would have to go because
there were no visitors allowed after 9:00 p.m. Her voice
was friendly. She said that we could come back tomorrow, but that she did not know if we would be allowed
to see Alice.

I texted Elisabeth to please come pick me up. Simon
offered to wait with me in the parking lot.

I said, "Thanks."

In the parking lot, I said, "Do you miss your dad?"

He looked at me with a flash of anger that disappeared
right away. "I do miss him, but I wish I didn't."

Then something strange happened. Instead of Elisabeth in the blue Smart car, Asparagus Man appeared,
driving his giant black equipment van. This was the
worst surprise. My guts began to pull in different directions. I got this powerful image of Alice dead on the
side of the road, even though she isn't dead. I was getting
irrational. What if Elisabeth was in an accident too?
What if she was the dead one?

I have finally gotten used to having Asparagus Man
around the house. I treat him like part of the scenery

that will disappear when we leave. I have made my peace. Still, the thought of riding beside him all alone was too much. Where the hell was my sister? What happened to her?

"Hey, Martin!" Asparagus Man called out through the window, all creepy-friendly. "Your sister went out to dinner with Arthur. So she asked me to grab you."

I froze.

"Ça va?" Simon asked me, meaning, "What's wrong?"

Instead of echoing back Ça va, I whispered, "Non, ça ne va pas."

"You don't want to get in the van with your mother's boyfriend?" he asked softly, so that Asparagus Man, who did not look impatient or uncomfortable, because he is so damn sure of himself, would not hear.

Simon got that Asparagus Man is Mom's boyfriend, when I'm still not even sure it's a fact. Since Layla has told me that moths are very detail-oriented about the lives of the people they orbit, I wasn't surprised Simon is clued in. So, Asparagus Man is Mom's boyfriend. This made me want to get into the van with him even less.

I stared at the tailpipe. It became my world. I would remember what it looked like for the rest of my life.

I don't know how long I stared. When Simon yelled, "Martin, wake up!" I looked at my watch to see that it was 9:31 p.m. "I'll come with you," Simon said. It's like his mom has strangers leaving shoes around his house and eating all his rhubarb jam, and he hates it as much as I do. "You get in the back, Martin, and I'll get in the front with him, okay?"

Then he said, in broken English, "Hi, Joe, I will come in the house of Martin with you in your camera truck."

"Fantastic," said Asparagus Man. "Samantha will be delighted to have you."

I wished I was the kind of kid who hits people.

On the ride home, Asparagus Man asked Simon about what had happened to Alice and how she was doing. He didn't bother to ask me.

When we got back to the cottage, Fuchsia was there, in the kitchen drinking red wine with Mom. "I'm so sorry to hear about your friend," Fuchsia said. Her eyes were extremely wide and moist. "Is she okay?" Her emotional response was appropriate in an exaggerated way, like a kid at The Center practicing concern.

As Simon told Fuchsia about Alice, her face moved along with his narrative, like a camera panning through a landscape. She bit her lower lip and furrowed her brow as much as she could through her Botox. Three times, she sighed.

Mom asked Simon if he could stay for dinner. She said

someone could give him a ride home later. He said he would love to. She asked him how he had enjoyed shooting the funeral scene at Chenonceau. He told her it had been very cool.

For dinner, we had couscous that Bernadette made, with lamb, carrots, zucchini, turnips, cabbage, tomatoes, and chickpeas.

After his first bite, Asparagus Man said, "This is great."

My body clenched.

Simon, who was sitting next to me, nudged me and whispered, "Don't think about it. Stay calm." Maybe he guessed that Papa loved couscous, and also that I wished Papa could be here eating it with us instead of Asparagus Man. And even if Simon didn't get all the specifics, he understood that I was missing my father. Simon is a gifted generalist. I admire him.

# Tuesday, June 21
## 6:00 p.m.

At 9:00 a.m., Simon texted to say that Alice's parents have asked us not to go to the hospital today. At first, I was scared this meant she was doing worse. So I called Simon. He promises she's getting better, but they don't want her to be stimulated yet because of the concussion. Her parents feel bad for us missing school for nothing. They hope we'll be able to see her tomorrow.

I texted Layla an update.

She sent me back a link to her new YouTube channel. I clicked on a line that said **For Martin**.

The screen opened to a close-up of her hands on the

piano. For a few seconds, her fingers rested on the keys. They trembled. Then they lit into notes I recognized instantly.

In secret, Layla has learned the musical phrase at the heart of my sonata. On her keyboard, she was playing the violin line, which is the melody. It's a miracle.

At first, I played the clip over and over in my room, watching her tiny wrists and big hands closely. After an hour, I took my phone into the hawthorn bushes. I stood there and listened to Layla, thinking of her and of Alice, and of the misunderstood composer of the sonata, Vinteuil. Mr. Swann knew Vinteuil personally but never put him together with this music. Vinteuil seemed way too ordinary to have done anything so beautiful.

Everything is mixing now. Layla, in faraway LA, has been reading *Search* and learning my music so that I can play it here in France in the bushes where I once felt the gaze of Gilberte, who is not Gilberte but Alice. All the elements of my life are streaming together. It should be very confusing. But it isn't. It's my madeleine.

Papa says that categories are way less absolute than we believe. His biggest hope for me is to stop being so categorical.

In my collection there's a postcard of a Flemish painting from 1670 by Pieter de Hooch. It's a woman, sitting by a cradle. And behind her, in a half-open doorway, is a little girl wearing a long white apron. Papa gave it to me because *Search* describes Mr. Swann's hearing the melody in the Vinteuil sonata like "those interiors by Pieter de Hooch which are deepened by the narrow frame of a half-opened door, in the far distance, of a different color, velvety with the radiance of some intervening light, the little phrase appeared, dancing, pastoral, interpolated, episodic, belonging to another world."

I found this postcard and I turned it over to the blank side. This is what I wrote:

> Dear Papa,
>
> I miss you and wish you were here to talk to me about a girl I have met who has been in an accident. I thought her name was Gilberte Swann at first, but it's really Alice Corot. This would be horrible if you hadn't worked so hard to teach me not to be too literal-minded. I hope you didn't confuse yourself while you were busy helping me out. I think about you all the time. It's because of you that I can be happy.
>
> Love, Martin

I screenshot the front and the back of the postcard and emailed it to Papa in jail. He will see it the next time he is allowed to check his email in the prison library.

Papa being in jail is my fault.

He was worried that I was too rigid and always putting things in categories. So he decided to teach me about the difference between fantasy and reality. He said that "in order to understand the nuances of reality," you have to be able to "dive into fantasy." You can't have one without the other. "They set each other off."

When we started out, he told me there was a real contrast between fantasy and reality, like black and white. But as he kept talking about it, he started thinking there wasn't such a major difference after all. That's when he got confused. He was trying to help me be less "literal-minded" and more "adaptable." He even started mixing up when parts of his investing work were real and when they were imagined. That's how badly he wanted me to get better.

It was the same with literal and figurative language. Papa told me that literal language tells things straight. Figurative language uses comparisons and metaphors. Most people get this difference on instinct, even if they don't have the fancy words to describe it. I had to learn it from Papa, with lots of examples from

*Search.* Like when Marcel stands in front of the haw-thorn bushes, breathing in their scent, he spends his time "losing and finding their invisible and fixed odor, uniting with the rhythm of their flowers, thrown here and there with a youthful joy and at unexpected inter-vals like certain musical intervals." Papa and I read that long sentence together about the hawthorn flowers and the musical intervals. We read it a bunch of times. He said he was realizing the flowers *were* the music, and the music *was* the flowers. I wasn't so sure about this, but I could tell he would be happy if I said that in the end there was no difference between figurative stuff and literal stuff. It would mean I was getting more flexible. So I agreed with him because he was doing his best.

We went through the same thing with style and sub-stance. When we baked the quatre-quarts cakes that drove Mom so crazy, Papa would always unmold them carefully from the pan so that they looked as perfect as possible. Julia Child said that "presentation is nine-tenths of the meal." The way you present something is as important as the thing itself. In fact, it *is* the thing it-self. Papa explained that to make a cake, we took style and substance and mixed them together, like we mixed together flour, butter, eggs, and sugar. We took our in-gredients and transformed them in the oven to make something new. "We merge style and substance into a single, beautiful baked good," he said.

This idea that there is no difference between the way things appear and the way they are was sometimes confusing to me. And it was very confusing to Papa. He lost sight of how money is not a metaphor. For most people, their money is very, very literal.

Papa did not plan to steal from his clients. He was sure he would make their money back eventually. When he lost it, he did not tell them. If they asked for their profits back, he paid them with money from other clients. For eight years, Papa hid this from his boss, Frank, who is an old friend from college. Frank let Papa work from home so that he could take care of me. Papa thought if he kept the right outlook, he would eventually make back enough money to pay everybody and make profits for Frank's small company, which is called a "boutique firm." He got caught. Frank went bankrupt.

Mom yelled at Papa, "Are you delusional?"

The family was in the kitchen. There was no question of cake-baking that day. Frank had just come over to tell us "exactly what has been going on" with the hiding of the lost money until it was too late to do anything about it. Papa apologized. He said it was complicated and he never meant for this to happen. Frank left in tears.

Papa argued to Mom that his behavior was a "form of optimism." He couldn't believe it all wasn't going to work out as long as he kept trying, which has always also been his attitude about me.

Mom repeated that he was delusional.

Elisabeth was also very angry at him. She screamed, "It wasn't like we needed the money! Why were you acting so desperate? Like you needed to steal to pay for Martin's care or something? What, are you nuts, Papa?"

He shrugged and looked at the floor.

Papa is not bad. He is good. He got delusional from spending too much time caring for a kid like me. By trying to loosen me up so that I could deal with the real world, he lost his own sense of it. The only other person who can see this is Layla. She has banked hundreds of hours of on-screen experience with characters clinging to irrational beliefs. So she knows exactly what I'm talking about.

There was a trial that lasted three months. Then Papa was sentenced to five years. I will be twenty when he gets out. I haven't been to visit him yet, but Elisabeth has promised to take me when we get home. The prison is a four-hour drive north of home.

The last time we were alone together, Papa and I had breakfast. We spent the whole morning talking about

Proust, which was much realer to us than that Papa was going to jail later that day. We went back to familiar places in the book. It made us comfortable. We ate the same thing we always eat for breakfast: toasted baguette with butter and rhubarb jam.

# Wednesday, June 22
## 5:10 p.m.

This morning, we were allowed back at the hospital. Elisabeth drove me again. We left at 9:00 a.m. Mom was long gone. She is into the final week of her shoot, so she is working almost all the time.

I asked Elisabeth to stop at the *boulangerie* on our way so that I could buy a bag of madeleines to give to Alice if they let me see her. I was so focused on giving the madeleines to her that I didn't even stop to worry about the male baker who was there instead of the usual woman in the pink apron. I forgot I get nauseated when I talk to strangers. I burst through the door and up to the counter.

I used to think that because I felt I already knew her, Alice was inside my bubble. Now I see that I'm someone who can fall in love outside myself.

When I got to the counter, I asked for six madeleines. Things seemed almost easy.

But if *Search* has taught me anything, it's that love is a struggle. When the baker asked me, *"Vous désirez autre chose?"* which means "Would you like something else?" I suddenly lost it.

*"Vous désirez autre chose?"* I echoed. I went on a loop. *"Vous désirez autre chose? Vous désirez autre chose? Vous désirez autre chose?"*

He interrupted me. *"Ça va?"*

Instead of answering him with a flat *Ça va*, I repeated his question back to him. *"Ça va? Ça va? Vous désirez autre chose?"*

Finally, I shut up and paid him. I even got out a *Merci*.

*"Merci!"* he shot back, laughing.

The madeleines were still warm.

In the car, I told Elisabeth about a time when Papa said to Mom that she shouldn't react so negatively when I repeated people's words back to them. I was twelve. He told her she was scaring me with her intensity, which was true.

He said, "Echolalia is not a moral failing."

Mom sighed. "You're right, it's not a moral issue, and I'm treating it like a moral issue." Then she admitted something, which doesn't happen a lot. "I'm scared for my son. When you're scared, you don't always think clearly."

"Believe me," Papa said, "I know."

When I was finished telling this to Elisabeth, she said, "I miss him too, Martin."

At 10:06, we arrived at the hospital. I told Elisabeth I could find my own way.

I didn't see Monsieur or Madame Corot in the waiting room. The moths had gone to school and wouldn't be here until late afternoon. This was my chance. I asked a nurse if I could see Alice. I was holding my bag of madeleines. I looked up from her clogs to her face so that she wouldn't decide I was strange. It was hard work, and it paid off.

The madeleines smelled buttery and sweet. The nurse looked down at the bag in my hands. She smiled. *"Ça sent bon,"* she said. Then she told me to follow her.

The nurse opened the door to Alice's room, which was very dimly lit. She was sitting up in bed, wearing an eye mask. Her face turned toward the sound of the door.

*"Maman?"* she asked. There was anxiety in her voice. It must be so scary to be blind.

"No," I said, "it's me, Martin."

The nurse watched Alice to make sure that she recognized my voice and that I wasn't some stranger pretending to be her friend. Alice smiled so bright that I was sure her eyes were sparkling under her blindfold.

"I wasn't sure you'd come," she said.

"Of course I'm here."

"I thought maybe . . ." She didn't finish.

I wasn't sure if I should touch her.

She reached out her hands, batting the air, searching. So I took her hands and gave her the paper bag to hold. Her hands were even softer than before, like they'd been resting.

"I brought you some madeleines," I said.

*"Merci,"* she said. Then she paused for a minute. "I'm sorry I left Simon's party without telling you. I couldn't find you. I was planning to come right back. Maybe you were disappointed? You had some idea of me that isn't true. Now you see I'm not that person."

"I do. And that's not a bad thing," I said. "And I'm not disappointed at all."

When she frowned, I said, "I'm sorry I threw up all over everyone."

"That's okay."

After that, we had trouble finding what to say, especially with the nurse standing there. Finally, I came up with, "So, does your head hurt?"

"A little. It's much better, though. I want to take this mask off, but I have to keep it on for another two days because of the concussion. Then I should be okay. My chest hurts because of my ribs, but that will go away."

"Do you want to hear our music?" I asked.

"Sure." She smiled.

I sat on the edge of her bed. I put one of my earbuds in her right ear and one in my left ear.

We listened. It was like we were coming home.

I forgot that the nurse was there until she interrupted us. "I'm sorry, but Alice needs to rest now," she said. "You'll have to go. You can come back later."

"I *am* resting!" Alice said. "Please let Martin stay. I'm so bored in here by myself." Her voice moved along with the music in our ears.

The nurse couldn't hear. "You can come back later."

"Wait! We haven't eaten our snack yet." Alice tried a new tactic. "Don't you want a madeleine, Martin?" She held the bag up in the air and moved it around like it was searching for me.

"Don't you want a madeleine, Martin? Yes, I want a madeleine, Alice," I answered, taking the bag.

We offered one to the nurse, who said no but that I could stay another few minutes.

I placed a madeleine in Alice's palm and watched as she gently folded her fingers around it. She held it for a second, touching it with her fingertips like braille. Then she ate it.

I ate one too.

Instead of handing her the next one, I held it up to her mouth and brushed her lips with it. She smiled and took a bite, licking the ends of my fingers. My fingers tingled.

"Delicious," she said.

I decided not to eat any more madeleines myself. I fed them all to her. I brushed her cheeks just below her blindfold and let her lick my fingers some more. My fingers felt bursting, like seedlings.

The nurse said I had to leave the room.

At 10:50 a.m., Alice's parents came into the waiting room with the baby in a stroller. Her mother wasn't wearing her soft sleeping clothes anymore. She was wearing long dark-green shorts and work boots with garden dirt on them. The dirt reminded me of Marcel shadowing Odette in the Bois de Boulogne, watching everyone whisper behind her. I used to dream of crossing Madame Corot's path, and now here she was saying hi to me and telling me to "come again tomorrow" because I obviously cheer Alice up. It was as if I had become friendly with the sun.

For the next two hours, I sat and read *Search* and listened to my music.

"I hope I'm more like Marcel than like Mr. Swann," I said to Elisabeth in the Smart car on our way home. It was 1:05 p.m.

"What do you mean?" she asked, but she was looking hard at the winding road and her voice was somewhere else.

"There's a big contrast between Marcel and Mr. Swann as far as their autism goes. Mr. Swann is stuck in his references. He can't get past them, and so he's always disappointed. Marcel uses references to imagine stuff. For him, names and places make his imagination go nuts. So he's not stuck. In his mind, he can go all over the place. This makes all the difference. Alice's life lets me imagine so many things."

"That's great, Martin."

I didn't detect sarcasm in her voice, but I did detect distraction. Elisabeth was not here. I got quiet. I wasn't unhappy.

## 11:45 p.m.

At home, Bernadette and I made ratatouille. She told me we had to cook the tomatoes, with the onions, at the beginning, so they lost their water. I've always added the tomatoes at the end. Now I get why my ratatouille has been soupy. Bernadette's is better. Only I wish she wouldn't dice her vegetables so small. She goes at them with a cleaver until they are tiny. I like chunks.

The people who ate the ratatouille, besides me and Bernadette, were Elisabeth, Arthur, and Mom. This list is important because Asparagus Man is not on it. Elisabeth and Arthur ate with me at 8:00 p.m. Then they went to a movie. At 9:20 p.m., Mom came home. I expected both doors of her car to open, but only the driver's door did, which was a relief because I haven't been able to talk to Mom all by myself for a long time.

Mom sat in the kitchen at the small table with the yellow-and-white-striped cloth and ate two bowls of ratatouille out of one of the green elephant-ear bowls that we also use for coffee in the morning.

"This is exactly what I need after my crazy day," she said. Then she smiled at me, the crinkling, not-tense smile. She said, "This is different from the ratatouille you make at home. It's thicker and richer. I like it."

"It's Bernadette's way. She taught me today. She cooks the tomatoes first instead of last."

"And you're okay with it not the same?"

"I like it."

"That's so wonderful! You and Bernadette cooking together! You guys have bonded, right?"

"Yeah," I answered. "Bernadette's cool."

"Oh, Martin, you are making so much progress!" She clapped her hands.

"You mean I'm getting more general-ed?"

As soon as I asked this, her smile changed to the one where her cheekbones pop because she is trying to manage a worry. She reached over and squeezed my hand. Her skin is dry, like soft paper.

"No, Martin. I'm sorry, that came out wrong. I don't want you to be general-ed. I want you to be happy. And you seem happier lately. That's all I mean. You're trying a new ratatouille recipe and you're trusting Bernadette in the kitchen, and you're making friends. It's all good, right? Are you happier? Is having a girl like Alice for a friend making you happier?"

"I don't know," I said. Then it hit me. "Getting close to Alice is making me realize how much I have to lose."

"You sound like your father," she said. I didn't hear bitterness. Her smile changed back to the real one again.

"Me like Papa? Is that bad? Or is that good?"

"I'm trying to state a fact the way you do, without judgment. I'm trying not to be such a perfectionist."

"I know it's my fault about Papa."

"What are you talking about?"

"Spending so much time with me made him delusional."

She started crying. Two slow tears down her cheeks. "Has your father ever made you feel like he would change anything about your time together?"

I thought for a moment. Then I shook my head.

"Of course he hasn't," she said. "Because he wouldn't give up a moment."

"But now he has to pay for me. That's not fair."

"I know it's hard to understand when you're a kid and it seems like everything is about you, but his crimes were separate from you. You can ask him. He'll tell you."

"Are you sure?"

"He was confused about finance. He wasn't confused about you at all."

I didn't quite follow her logic, but the tone of her voice was so sure that I felt forgiven.

"I need to talk this over with Layla," I said, because Layla knows better than anyone how I feel about Papa.

There were two more tears. "Layla loves you very

much, Martin. She doesn't want you to move on with-out her. It's completely natural. But you don't belong in a bubble with her anymore."

She put her face in her hands. "Oh, God, I sound so cruel!"

"But I am not only in Layla's bubble. I'm other places too."

"What places?"

"Other places. Inside and outside of different bubbles. It doesn't only have to be one thing. I think other people have this too."

"You mean, other people have bubbles? Is that what you're saying?"

"Yes! That's it. Like Papa. And me. And you." I was ex-cited. "People, all people, can be inside and outside them at the same time. So I don't have to abandon Layla. I don't have to get a new face. Getting a new face is not the same thing as growing up."

"No, it's not. And I love your face."

I hugged her, and she kept crying. "Mom," I said, "I think, I think—"

"You think you're going to be okay."

"Yes," I said.

# Friday, June 24
## 10:15 p.m.

Papa has taught me that an inference is an "opinion or idea we form based on evidence and clues, in reading and in life."

When I told Alice today that Layla wants her to hear our sonata played on The Center's piano, I was somewhere between an inference and a lie. Layla never said to play her music for Alice. But I wish she would.

This afternoon, at 4:30, Alice got to take her blindfold off, and I decided to show her Layla's hands on my phone to celebrate. I also brought a big bag of madeleines into the hospital, enough for the whole gang.

At 5:30 p.m., we were allowed into Alice's room. We crowded around her on her bed, drinking Oranginas and eating the madeleines. I said to Alice, "My friend Layla from Los Angeles, the one who draws the moths on my shoes, she sent us something." I held up my phone for her. Simon and the others looked too.

I pressed the play arrow. After a few seconds of Layla's hands on the keyboard, Alice's eyes widened. I was watching her eyes to see if they match up with my memory of them from before the blindfold. They do. They're the same soft brown. They're beautiful.

The other kids weren't as into it as us. The César Franck sonata means nothing to them because they don't recognize it. It's between Alice and me. And Layla, of course. Without Layla, I could never have gotten to know Alice. I would not have had enough belief.

After the music, Simon asked if I was happy about going home to California soon. He said I must miss my life in LA, and all my friends and my mom's Hollywood crowd.

Before I could answer, Alice asked, "When are you leaving?"

"In three days," I said.

Everyone stared at me. Normally, I'm very clear about

timing. But I haven't said anything about leaving France. Probably because I have been trying to keep it out of my own mind.

"Wow, you could have told us. This stupid town won't even seem real to you when you go back to your normal life," Simon said.

"That's not true at all," I said. "I'll remember everything."

This made them laugh. They made me promise to come back before we all get too old to recognize one another. Definitely before the end of high school. Then they said I probably wouldn't come back.

They're not kidding. This moment can't last. We all get it.

At 6:00 p.m., the nurse made us leave Alice's room. She's getting out of the hospital tomorrow morning. Then Monday she'll be back at school. I'll go to school too. Then, the next morning, I'll take a train to Paris, with Elisabeth and Mom, and then we'll fly home to LA.

On my way out of the hospital, I got this text from Layla: When you get home, how would you like to come over and watch Season Five with me? How about next Friday? The summer session doesn't start until after July 4. You are coming to the summer session, right?

The Center runs all year so that we don't regress.

I texted back: I will be there for the summer session. And yes, I would like to watch Season Five together very much. Thank you for asking.

I thought about telling her I am sorry I made her jealous and that her learning the sonata is a big deal, and that I am grateful for the way our brains can touch. I realized I don't need to say it. What I need to do is go sit with her on the brown couch.

# Saturday, June 25
## 7:00 p.m.

Papa answered my email.

Dear Martin,

Thanks for your picture of the postcard. I love the part in *Search* about the melody being like a doorway. It's great to hear from you. I'm sorry it has taken me a few days to write back. As you know, I don't have access to a computer that often. Twice a week for half an hour, to be exact. I'm happy to hear about Alice Corot. I hope she is okay. I'd love more details about her if you have the time and the inclination. I can tell that you are making great use of *Search* in its native land.

I'm sure Mom has told you that we have decided to get a divorce. Partly it is to protect assets for you and your sister. I am getting sued by a lot of people, so it's best to divide up what we have so that your mother's portion is safe and she can use it for you and Elisabeth. Mom is ready to move on, and I want you to know it is not your fault. You said to me once that you are worried you confused me. You didn't confuse me. I confused myself. But we are all going to be okay. You say I've helped you learn to be happy, and I hope that this serves you well now.

By the time I get out of here, you will be a master baker. I hope you will still bake a quatre-quarts with your old man for old times' sake. I promise to clean up.

Love you, Papa

When I was a kid and I heard something I didn't like, I stated the opposite. Like if Elisabeth said she had hurt herself, I said, "Elisabeth did not hurt herself. Elisabeth is okay." Or if Mom said it was raining, so we couldn't go to the park, I said, "It's not raining. We can go to the park." Or if Papa said he was sad because of something terrible that happened in the newspaper, I yelled, "Papa is not sad! Papa is happy!"

The therapists said these contradictions were not exactly original speech, but they were "something."

Eventually, they taught me I couldn't make things the way I wanted them to be. It's not appropriate to believe in that kind of power once you aren't a baby anymore. Only it took me until I was ten and a half to stop trying. Even now, if something messes with my vision of reality, I have a hard time. I block painful things, like Asparagus Man and the divorce. Mom's tried to tell me about the divorce four times. I haven't contradicted her. I also haven't said I get it. And I haven't told anyone else.

Until today.

I went to see Alice. She was sitting outside in a white plastic chair in the yard of her house, which is the same square shape and size as Simon's yard. She was wearing cut-off shorts, a striped T-shirt, and sunglasses. Except for the bandage on her head, she looked the same as before. She was drinking a tall glass of sparkling water with dark-green mint syrup in it. She offered me some, but

I said no thanks. I don't like mint. She said she felt fine, and then she asked how I was.

I told her about the divorce and about Papa in jail.

Alice said she was sorry. But she did not seem shocked. She made me feel normal. Then she asked me a question.

"Because your brain works differently, is it harder for you than for other kids to think about your dad and your parents splitting up? Harder to accept?"

"Sometimes," I said, "I don't grasp certain things the way other people do. It's like I don't live in quite the same world."

"Okay, I need to say something to you," she said. She was narrowing her eyes in a way that reminded me of Gilberte even though I'm now completely sure that Alice is not Gilberte. Gilberte would never have a green sparkle from her drink in the soft hair above her lip. "You tell me that you live in this different world because of your Proust book and how your mind works and everything. And you make it seem that all of us here are kind of privileged because we don't have to live in your world. Like you might be trapped, and we are free. What you don't get is that you're rich and you live in America and you hang out with famous people and you don't even notice that that makes you lucky. You're gonna go away from here and have a million things happen to you. We're the ones who are trapped. Not you."

"I'm sorry," I said, before I could process, because an apology is appropriate when you've offended someone, even before you figure out why. Then I had an idea. "Maybe you're saying we have something in common?"

"No, the opposite. I'm saying we don't."

"But we do. We both know the other one is lucky."

We talked for another ten minutes, but we didn't get anywhere. She kept saying my life was glamorous and I would forget her, and I kept saying I could never forget. She started to act like our argument was a game. She was laughing and giving silly examples about how she pictured my "Hollywood life" in Jacuzzis with champagne and movie stars. It was so silly that she relaxed, so I relaxed. We held hands.

I was hoping we would kiss, but Madame Corot came out of the house to say it was almost dinnertime and Alice should come eat. There was a strong smell of frying steak through the door to the house, and it made me hungry. I wanted to stay and eat, but Madame Corot didn't invite me. So I took a long, winding walk home while the sun was setting.

On the way, I stopped to text Layla. **Do we live in a bubble of privilege along with our other bubbles?**

She answered, **Privilege can be confused with glamour, but it is not the same thing. Do you think our phones are instruments of communication or torture?**

I thought about Layla's parents throwing money at the problem that was her, and about Papa being in jail for trying to solve the problem that is me, and I started to cry on the side of the road. I don't want so much separation from people. Not from Alice, not from Layla, not from the moths, not from my family.

I was going to text Layla to please give me a song, but before I could, she sent me another link to her YouTube channel. She was playing the Beatles' "I Will."

# Sunday, June 26
## 4:00 p.m.

Mom and Asparagus Man have broken up. It happened two days ago. Elisabeth told me this afternoon. She said that she didn't know why and that Mom didn't want to talk about it. My first feeling surprised me. It was not the rush of relief and well-being I expected.

When I heard, I called Maeva. She has given me her cell number for emergencies. She picked up even though it was 6:00 a.m. her time, and she did not sound groggy. She was happy to hear from me.

I told her right away that I was worried my mom

might be sad. I explained that she and the man she had been dating here had broken up.

"What is he like?" she asked.

"Well, I'm not sure what he is really like, but to me he is kind of a nightmare."

"So aren't you glad he's out of the picture?"

"But it's not my picture," I said. "It's her picture. What if she is sad?"

"Does she seem sad?"

"No, she seems busy. But Elisabeth said she sometimes hides in her work."

"How do you think you can find out how she's really doing?"

"I can ask her?"

"That's the best you can do."

### 6:35 p.m.

Arthur has shaved. I am trying to be cool about it, but it's rocking my world. I like him. I've come beyond identifying him as a tangle of fur with eyes and a smile. Still, he is scaring me with all his skin, like a brand-new creature. It's a lot at once.

Elisabeth can tell I'm having a hard time with the

change. She asks if it's related to anxiety about leaving Chenonceaux and returning to LA, where everything might not feel the same as it did before we left. Because I might not be the same. These are interesting questions, but I forget all about them when Arthur's pale white face makes me nervous.

I try to focus on his familiar voice instead of his smooth new skin. It's late afternoon. We're taking a walk along the edge of the castle garden, by the river. I'm counting the six arches across the water, and their six reflections, which make six perfect ovals.

Over my steady counting, I can hear what he says. He asks me, "What are you going to do for the rest of the summer, once you get home?"

"Well, I'll go to summer school at The Center, and also take some classes at a general-ed school to see if there's any way I could go there next year. I don't think I want to but I am trying to be flexible. And I'll swim every day with my team. And I'll probably cook and read a lot."

"Are you psyched to see Layla?" Elisabeth asks.

I count all six ovals again before I answer her.

"Yeah, I want her to draw me some more moth sneakers because these ones are worn out. And I am also worried about seeing her."

"Why?"

"Because you might have hurt her feelings," I say. "You think you and she understand what happened now. It should be okay but it might be hard."

Elisabeth does a sharp inhale, as if she is going to say, "Pronoun alert!" She doesn't say anything.

It's Arthur who talks. "Are you going to see her?" he asks.

"You can't *not* do hard things," I say.

Before heading to bed, I tell Elisabeth that I'll be able to look at Arthur's new face soon. She says he's going to spend the summer in LA to help Mom edit the movie. So we will see him a lot. I ask what will happen between them when she goes to Stanford, and she says she can't predict, but not in a sad way. Then she asks if I am going to do something special with Alice to say good-bye. I say my friends are going to come to the train station on Tuesday. Alice too.

Elisabeth doesn't try to make me say any more about Alice, and I'm grateful. I haven't kissed Alice since her accident, and all I want is another chance before I go.

# Tuesday, June 28
## 5:30 p.m.

In the last scene of *Swann's Way*, Marcel is walking in the Bois de Boulogne, stalking Odette, while all these men are whispering around her. Marcel is two people at once. He is the innocent, starstruck boy who is mesmerized by Odette, the glamorous mother of Gilberte. And he is also the old writer imagining what all the men are saying about the woman he has idolized from afar. Young Marcel tips his hat to the great lady in a ridiculous, romantic way that makes her smile. Then the scene drifts forward in time to Marcel as an old man. He's still wandering through the Bois de Boulogne. Only the park has lost all of its artful magic and become an ordinary, natural place. Like if the perfect Chenonceau gardens got reclaimed by wild grasses and nobody trimmed the trees anymore. The horses with their carriages have been replaced by cars. The women's fashions are completely changed and seem strange to Marcel. Instead of elegant little hats with fresh flowers, the women are wearing giant hats with heavy decorations. And instead of the beautiful, structured dresses that made Odette look like a queen, they're wearing shapeless Liberty-print frocks that look like cheap wallpaper.

This makes Marcel realize something: an image in our heads is nothing but regret for a certain moment. All the things we think exist outside of us, like houses and roads and avenues through the park, are "as fleeting as the years." They aren't real.

It is 5:35 p.m. You are sitting in seat forty-five of a train speeding through fields between the Loire Valley and Paris, in a second-class carriage because traveling first class is vulgar. Right now, the fields are sunflower and beet. You are going over images in your head, trying to decide if they are fleeting or not.

Here is a list of the images:

The orange doorways at school. They are no longer startling blurs along an endless hallway. You can now picture what is behind them: the classrooms, the cafeteria, the gym. Alice can be found behind the doorway to French and history. She is also often behind the door to the cafeteria. At your last school lunch, she makes you a surprise, a big slice of quatre-quarts cake with a moth drawn on it in Nutella. She has decorated the wings with banana slices. It is beautiful.

In Simon's backyard last night, the table has a bowl of chips, some cans of soda, some beers, and a box of wine. There is no techno music. There is a circle of shoes, bodies, faces. Simon, Kevin, Marianne, Georges, Michel, and Alice are your *petit clan*. You are here with them to say good-bye instead of back on the cottage terrace with the cast and crew. Good-bye is something you haven't practiced nearly as much as you've practiced greeting. It isn't natural yet. You stand there holding your beer, smiling vaguely in everyone's direction. You have the will, but you don't know what to do with it.

Simon says that you are truly cool for a robot. He doesn't have to ask if you understand he's joking because you laugh, and you're not angry at all anymore. And you say maybe there will be a premiere of Mom's movie in Paris and we can all go be moths together, and he lights up because he's a moth like you're a robot.

Alice is wearing a black cotton T-shirt dress with straps crisscrossing the back. It looks like the dresses Elisabeth wears for lyrical dance class. Her arms are wiry, like yours. She takes both your hands and says, "Come on, let's go to the other side of the house."

There is a kiss. The old strangeness from the first kisses is gone. There is the new strangeness of knowing it will never be like this anymore.

You say to her, "I can't believe I ever wanted you to be someone else. I hate it when people want *me* to be someone else. I'm sorry." And she says it's okay, but that she doesn't want to talk about it because it will make her sad. This is when you understand that she is as sad as you are.

This morning, you swim laps in town. You memorize the bottom of the pool, the six black tile lines, the seven major cracks.

You have a late breakfast on the terrace with Mom, Elisabeth, and Fuchsia. There are croissants and rhubarb jam. After Fuchsia leaves and Elisabeth goes to brush her teeth, you ask Mom if she is okay about breaking up with Asparagus Man. She says it was never serious, and she could tell you didn't like him, so she thought you would be relieved. Then she gives you a deep, crinkled smile. "Wow, Martin, your first thought was for your old mother?" she asks. You nod. "But you're not old," you say.

When Bernadette kisses you good-bye on both cheeks, you do not flinch.

You pack your postcard collection.

The flies are giving their same concert.

Asparagus Man is not doing dishes.

Arthur is on the train platform kissing Elisabeth good-bye, saying he will see her in LA in a few days.

Your friends are on the platform too. They have ditched school this afternoon to say good-bye. They are waving and shouting and taking pictures with their phones as the train pulls away. They will not see you in LA in a few days.

Alice hands you a bag of madeleines. *"Ça va?"* she asks, meaning, "Are you ready?" *"Ça va,"* you answer. You would love to save the madeleines, but this is not a good idea because they will get stale. Trying to save them will only make you lose them eventually. So you eat them slowly, one after the other, while the fields of beets and sunflowers go by.

Elisabeth is wearing her hawthorn dress on the train. Mom is sleeping.

You don't feel like an old man full of regrets who longs

after past styles of hats or Doc Martens. You feel like I do. Like you are at the very beginning of your life. Things are always changing, but there is also a solid place that is you. A place where the people you love are not fleeting. A place where you, Martin, in seat forty-five at 6:03 p.m., are I.

# Acknowledgments

**K**ids like Us has been wildly lucky in its readers along the way. You have meant the world to me.

Thank you to my brilliant agent, Stéphanie Abou, and to the amazing Joy Peskin at FSG. You both inspire me with the courage of your convictions.

For their generous red pens, I am grateful to Sarah Burnes, Ellie Garland, Logan Garrison, John Gill, Bob Gottlieb, Shireen Harri, Rachel Knecht-Scher, Hannah Nordhaus, Eleanor O'Neill, Margie Stohl, Amor Towles, and John Wyatt.

For their enthusiastic reads and encouraging words, thanks to Dyanne Asimow, Micheline Barthe, Katherine

Blackmon, Keli Block, Elisabeth Boger, Ann Brashares, Jasie Britton, Katie Browning, Maude Chilton, Jim Clayson, Nick Cloke, Susan Cloke, Gretchen Crary, Melissa de la Cruz, Nancy Danahoe, Stephanie Douglass, Emily Eakin, Monique El-Faizy, Hilary Garland, Dave Gilbert, Lizzie Gottlieb, Claudia Grazioso, Jon Hall, Julia Hall, Latifa Hamiani, Phoebe Herms, Joanna Hershon, Lindita Iasilli, Sara Lebow, Ben Lieberman, Ann Mah, Linda Marini, Seema Merchant, Bonnie Moses, Maureen O'Neill, Kirsten O'Reilly, Maggie Parker, Joanne Ramos, Caroline Reyl, Dominique Reyl, Eldine Reyl, Francois Reyl, Olivia Reyl, Rafi Simon, Anjali Singh, Bennett Stein, Kimbrough Towles, Maggie Towles, and Fionna Watt.

Tess O'Neill, I treasure the moth sneakers you made for me.

Many thanks to Penny Hueston and Michael Heyward at Text Publishing and Caspian Dennis at Abner Stein for taking Martin around the world.

Thank you to Charles, the light of my life and my model for persistence, and to my terrific daughters, Ella, Iris, and Margaux.

Finally, thanks to my mother and father, Harriet and Tim Whelan, whose optimism is everywhere in this book, and to my wonderful sister, Eleanor O'Neill. You are the most hopeful of all.